Anonymous

The Life of Mrs. Abington

formerly Miss Barton - celebrated comic actress, with full accounts of her

various performances in the theatres of London and Dublin

Anonymous

The Life of Mrs. Abington
formerly Miss Barton - celebrated comic actress, with full accounts of her various performances in the theatres of London and Dublin

ISBN/EAN: 9783337334123

Printed in Europe, USA, Canada, Australia, Japan

Cover: Foto ©Andreas Hilbeck / pixelio.de

More available books at **www.hansebooks.com**

THE LIFE OF

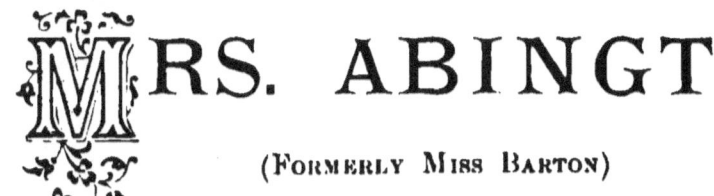RS. ABINGTON

(FORMERLY MISS BARTON)

CELEBRATED COMIC ACTRESS,

WITH

Full Accounts of her Various Performances in the Theatres of London and Dublin.

INCLUDING ALSO INTERESTING

NOTES UPON THE HISTORY OF THE IRISH STAGE

AND COPIOUS NOTICES, ANECDOTES, AND CRITICISMS OF HER THEATRICAL CONTEMPORARIES.

Embellished with a Portrait in Steel after Cosway.

BY THE EDITOR OF THE "LIFE OF QUIN."

LONDON:

READER, ORANGE STREET, HOLBORN.

1888.

PREFACE.

THE following " Life of Mrs. Abington, formerly Miss Frances or Fanny Barton," is sent forth in full confidence of a hearty welcome by the public.

This celebrated lady achieved so high a position in the comic walks of theatrical life, and was so famed for her personal beauty and exquisite taste in those matters of dress which are so dear to the female heart, that anything like a consecutive narrative of her career must be of general interest. Hitherto, all that has appeared in print, has been of such a disjointed and fragmentary, as well as limited, character, that it was exceedingly difficult to get anything like a clear idea of the origin, progress, and successful termination of her professional life; an effort has now been made, after considerable labour and research, to connect and arrange in chronological order, all attainable and trustworthy facts.

Very full lists are given of the parts she played in various comedies, &c., on the stages of the London and Dublin theatres, and, to relieve these from the barrenness and dryness naturally attending them, many of their characteristics have been dwelt upon, and, so far as was necessary and proper to the faithful exhibition of Mrs. Abington's experience and influence, incidental notices of other performers and historical notes respecting the Irish stage have been freely added.

Under these circumstances the publisher believes that the book will be peculiarly acceptable to those who have read some of the brief references to this actress's life which have occasionally appeared, and who have had neither the time nor the facilities for the search and study necessary to the construction of a reliable biography.

The Life of Mrs. Abington.

—⊱⋇⊰—

CHAPTER I.

Mrs. Abington's Ancestors—Her Parents—Struggles for a Living—
Obscurity of Early Life—Out at Service—New and Questionable
Acquaintances at Golden Square—Resolves to be an Actress—Early
Attempts at the Haymarket Theatre—At Bath—At Richmond—
Appearance in her real Name at Drury Lane—Appearances in Plays of
Double Dealer, Cato, Winter's Tale, Squire of Alsatia, Mock Doctor,
Zara, Heiress—Illness of Mrs. Clive, Miss Barton takes her place—Plays
in the Rehearsal, Beggar's Opera, Mourning Bride, Careless Husband,
Old Man taught Wisdom, Guardian, The Wonder, Arden of Faversham—
Marries and appears in Romeo and Juliet, as Mrs. Abington—Difficulties
at Drury Lane, owing to surplus of Actresses, irregularity of her
engagements—Last Appearances on the London Stage in the Stratagem,
Conscious Lovers, Suspicious Husband, Old Man taught Wisdom, Double
Gallant, Way of the World—Lying Valet, High Life Below Stairs—
Rupture with her Husband—Jealousy of the Actors and Actresses.

The celebrated and beautiful woman whose life and experiences
are here chronicled, was, like many of her class and profession,
of extremely humble origin. It is said, indeed, that she was
descended from a family of some distinction in the Reign of
William the Third, the head of which was then Christopher
Barton, Esq., of Norton, Derbyshire, who, at his death left four
sons, one a colonel, one a ranger of the royal parks, another an
ecclesiastic of Westminster, and a younger one who was her
grandfather; for all this, however, her parents moved but in a
lowly condition of life, her father being only a cobbler, keeping
a small stall in Vinegar Yard, and her brother an ostler of the
most inferior type, in Stanway Yard.

According to some, Frances Barton (which was our heroine's
name) never knew her mother, but earlier accounts tell us that
she had the misfortune to lose her maternal relation when she
was about fourteen years of age. Be this as it may, it is agreed
on all hands that from a very early age she experienced most

severely the want of a mother's care and guidance, and led a life, in every particular, likely to prove disastrous. The father's trade was but a poor one, and sometimes down-right starvation was staring them in the face, there being neither food nor money in the house to supply their most ordinary wants. The consequence was that the motherless girl was sent out to earn a few pence in whatever way she could, to assist in procuring the bare necessaries of life. She sold flowers, she went on errands, she sang and recited at public houses, in short, did all kinds of things by which a trifle could be earned to add to the slender resources of home. Occasionally, by the aid of a kindly disposed waiter, she would, upon earnest application, obtain admission to the better class of houses, such as the Bedford or the Shakspeare, in the Piazza, Covent Garden, when to the company met in the private rooms of those establishments she would from a stage extemporised from a table, recite various passages from the poets, her efforts and beauty winning the reward of a few pence from her auditors.

This Fanny or Frances Barton, was born either in the year 1731 or 1737, which of the two, it is impossible to say, as the few records of her life extant, differ considerably. In her earlier days, while wandering about London endeavouring to earn something to ward off the pangs of hunger and starvation, and when known as "Nosegay Fan," no attempt was made to establish an ancestry superior in station to that of her parents, but when afterwards she had reached a position of eminence and prosperity, it was thought advisable to ascertain from what kind of a stock she had sprung, and the result was the discovery of the pedigree we have mentioned.

More than a hundred years ago a magazine contributor wrote, "In attempting a portrait of this celebrated comic actress, we lament with Cibber, 'that the animated graces of the player can live no longer than the instant breath and motion that present them; or at least can but faintly glimmer through the memory or imperfect attestation of a few surviving spectators.'"

In her memoirs, however, we shall be able to hold up to posterity the early and rapid strides she made in her profession; and from the various and contrasted characters she appeared in with unrivalled applause, they will at least be able to conclude with certainty, "that Mrs. Abington was the first comic actress of her time." None of the present day, for instance, can remember Betterton, and consequently can know nothing personally of the abilities of this once celebrated tragedian, but who can read this declaration of Cibber "that he never heard a line in tragedy come from Betterton, wherein his judgment, his ear, and his imagination, were not fully satisfied, but must rest perfectly convinced of his transcendent abilities."

Considerable obscurity hangs over a greater portion of the early life of Miss Barton, and it is with difficulty we are able to trace her various movements and occupations. While still very young, she seems to have become a servant in the house of a milliner, in Cockspur Street, where she acquired the beginnings of that taste in dress which afterwards brought her so much celebrity, and also her knowledge of the French language. At another time she was maid in a kitchen whose cook was Mrs. Baddelay, who, after filling the same office in the houses of Lord North, Mr. Foote, and others, and that of travelling *valet de chambre*, ultimately became a popular performer of foreign parts, footmen, Jews and broken English.

A modern writer has told us that "Fanny underwent many painful and ignoble experiences, that her early days were miserable, squalid and vicious, but that she strove after a better life. She may not be judged with severity, at least the circumstances of her condition must be remembered in passing sentence upon her, and something of the evil of her career must be charged to the heartlessness of the world in which she lived. "Low, poor and vulgar as she had been," a contemporary critic writes, "she was always anxious to acquire education and knowledge. It was understood that she was well acquainted with the French authors, could read and speak French with facility, and could converse in Italian." Her rise from obscurity to distinction, from wretchedness to prosperity, was a task of exceeding difficulty, and she had but herself and her own efforts to depend upon. But by dint of industry, indomitable courage and great natural intelligence she triumphed at last, she struggled desperately with the world, but she tore success from it in the end.*

Shortly after losing her mother, who seems to have been a woman of considerable knowledge for her station, as well as a tender and indulgent parent, Fanny, or Frances, was taken into the house of a female relation of her father's, in Sherrard Street, Golden Square, where she continued nearly three years, her vivacity and engaging manners making her the favourite of all who had the pleasure of her acquaintance and the "promised blessing of a future comfort to her family."

About this period a young lady from Bath, came, under a particular recommendation, to board in the same house, where she soon commenced an intimacy with young Frances, whom

*D. Cook.

she used to take frequently with her to see plays, and communicated an intention of going upon the stage, advising the other to do the same, as a more preferable state than that of depending on any friend or relation, informing her that she had interest enough to introduce her to the same manager she was then in treaty with, and doubted not of her succeeding. The proposal did, by no means, displease our young heroine; and from that moment the desire of commencing actress was her constant and utmost wish.

While this project was carrying on, Miss Barton's relation discovered that her boarder from Bath was not the most circumspect of Diana's train, and had been carrying on an intrigue with a favourite Endymion for a considerable time with the greatest secrecy, even from her young female companion. On warning being given her to seek for other lodgings, she prevailed on Frances to quit her friend's house, the better to effect the plan of going on the stage together;—but gallantries being prevalent in the mind of this fair monitor, she went off with her inamorato and left the decoyed young Frances (whose friends she had deserted) to shift for herself in the best manner she could. In this situation she consulted with her abilities to know in what form of exertion they might most effectually rescue her from the state in which her fair friend had left her. The profession of actress presented itself anew to her, as the most flattering prospect, as well as the most practicable, and very soon a favourable opportunity presented itself for making an essay. The late Mr. The. Cibber, son of Colley Cibber, Esq., poet laureate, a comedian of eminence in his days of prosperity, had obtained a licence from the Lord Chamberlain to exhibit plays for a certain number of nights at the theatre in the Haymarket, to which theatre Miss Barton was invited, to make her first appearance. The character she attempted was that of Miranda, in "The Busy Body," which she executed with such an amazing spirit and propriety, that she received the compliments of several acknowledged connoisseurs in theatrical affairs, who had been present during the whole exhibition. From that night her alliance proved of great emolument to this occasional manager, and which he ever after most gratefully acknowledged. She afterwards appeared as Miss Jenny, in "The Provoked Husband;" as Kitty Pry, in "The Lying Valet;" as Sylvia, in "The Recruiting Officer;" as Prince Prettyman, in "The Rehearsal;" and as Mrs. Tattoo, in "Lethe." Young as she was and a mere novice in the profession, she also played the character of Desdemona with so much applause, that the late Mr. Shuter, who had seen her in tragedy and comedy, came behind the scenes and engaged her for Mr. Simpson, proprietor of the Bath theatre, at that time under the management of Mr. King. Having gone through the Bath seasons (there were two in each year) with increasing promise and reputation, Miss Barton returned to London, and Mr. Shuter eagerly sought to find her and enlisted her to join the light corps of comedians selected from the two London theatres to play at Richmond during the summer. There Mr. Lacy saw her perform frequently and was so pleased with her acting the first night that he was present that he invited her to visit his family at Isleworth, and engaged her for Drury Lane playhouse, where she continued for a season, daily gaining popularity and public favour.

Her first appearance at this theatre was on the 29th October, 1756, as Lady Pliant in "The Double Dealer," with the following cast :

Maskwell	MOSSOP.
Sir Paul Pliant	FOOTE.
Brisk	WOODWARD.
Careless	PALMER.
Lady Touchwood	MRS. PRITCHARD.
Lady Froth	MRS. CLIVE.
Lady Pliant	MISS BARTON.

On this occasion her name was concealed from the public and her character was announced in the bills as to be played by a " young gentlewoman appearing for the first time." On the 10th of the following month she was advertised as Miss Barton, and was engaged to perform in a number of small parts in all of which she managed to give considerable satisfaction both to her employers and to the public.

Amongst other parts, she took a small one in a play called Cato, written by Foote, a piece which brought him into a good deal of trouble. The cast of Cato was as follows :

Cadwallader	FOOTE.
Young Cape	ROSS.
Vamp (a bookseller)	YATES.
Sprightly	USHER.
Governor Cape	BRANSBY.
Mrs. Cadwallader	MRS. CLIVE.
Arabella (sister to Cadwallader)	MISS BARTON.

"Young Cape believes his father to be dead—he has turned author to support himself—he is in love with Arabella, but has little or no hopes of obtaining her brother's consent to their union—Cadwallader is very proud of his pedigree—Mrs. Cadwallader is a fool—at the conclusion Governor Cape discovers himself to be young Cape's father—young Cape marries Arabella. Foote's part was admirably acted, and Mrs. Clive was nowise inferior; the performance of these two popular artistes gave the piece a great run.

Cadwallader was meant for Mr. Apreece, a gentleman of fortune and family with whom Foote was very intimate, a circumstance which was so far from restraining the wantonness of Foote's pen, that it only served to give him the readiest means of finishing his picture with the greatest exactness. Foote took care to have Mr. Apreece as one of the audience— that gentleman at first joined in the general laugh at his own portrait, but at last the joke became so serious that he applied to the Lord Chamberlain (Cooke), and obtained the suppression of the piece."

In 1757 (March 24), we find her performing, for Woodward's benefit, in "The Winter's Tale," with the following cast :

Leontes	GARRICK.
Daffodil	WOODWARD.
Tukely	PALMER.
Dizzy	YATES.
Sophia	MISS MACKLIN.
Arabella	MISS MINORS.
Mrs. Dotterel	MISS BARTON.
Widow Damply	MISS CROSS.
Lady Fanny Pewit...	MRS. BRADSHAW.

In October of the same year she played Lady Pliant in the "Double Dealer" with Blakes as Lord Froth.

In 1758, on May 2nd, was performed "The Squire of Alsatia," which had not been acted for ten years, Miss Barton taking the part of Mrs. Termagant. Cast as follows :

Squire	WOODWARD.
Sir William Belford	YATES.
Belford, Junior	HAVARD.
Mrs. Termagant	MISS BARTON
Isabella	MRS. CLIVE.
Ruth	MRS. MACKLIN.
Mrs. Hackum	MRS. BRADSHAW.

On the 8th of May she played the part of Dorcas, in "The Mock Doctor," with Yates as Gregory.

On the 13th of November she played Foible in " The Way of the World," on the 17th Lady Pliant in " The Double Dealer," and, on the 20th of December, Rhodamintha in " Zara," for the benefit of the General Lying-in Hospital.

Feeble (and old debauchee) ...	YATES.
Felix (his son)	OBRIEN.
Sir William Wheedle (a sharper).	PALMER.
Mrs. Furbelow	MRS. BENNET.
Rhodamintha (her daughter) ...	MISS BARTON.
Lady Never-Settle	MISS PRITCHARD.

" Feeble is in love with Rhodamintha—he intends to marry her, and only wants to be satisfied that she is a gentlewoman— Mrs. Furbelow, by the suggestion of Sir William, who is her confederate, gives a Rout—several persons are engaged to assume the appearance of noblemen—at the conclusion, Felix convinces his father that Mrs. Furbelow and her daughter are women of infamous character—this F. had been announced in the preceding bills, as being written by a person of quality—it is on the whole, a poor piece—Lady Never-Settle is a short character, but a very good one. (Genest.)

On the 21st of May, 1759, was acted at Drury Lane, the " Heiress," or " Antigallican," with the following cast :

Captain Hardy (the Antigallican)... ...	YATES.
Dash (a Coxcomb)	PALMER.
Briton, senior	BURTON.
Briton, junior (his Son)	PACKER.
Harriot (the Heiress, disguised as a Boy)	Miss BARTON.
Letitia (Daughter to Briton)	Miss HIPPISLEY.
Mrs. Spruce (a Milliner)	MRS. BRADSHAW.
Lady Everbloom	MRS. SIMPSON.

The dialogue of this Farce is not bad—the plot is very slight —Harriot, for family reasons has been brought up as a boy— Letitia falls in love with Harriot, supposing her to be a man— at the conclusion, Harriot's sex is discovered, and she is united to Briton, junior. Thomas Moseen, the actor, published this piece in a volume of poems, in 1762, he says that the character of Harriot was objected to as unnatural—so it is—but a similar character had been introduced by two of our best writers—by Fletcher, in " Love's Cure," and by Vanburgh, in "The Mistake." (Genest.)

This was the first "breeches" part undertaken by Miss Barton. Shortly after, Mrs. Clive appears to have been incapacitated by illness from taking her usual place on the Drury Lane stage, and Miss Barton, in consequence, was deputed to play several of her characters.   On May 25th, 1759, she played a small part in "The Rehearsal" with Garrick as Bayes; on May 28th, she played Melissa in the "Beggar's Opera" with the Lying Valet; on May 29th, she played Charlotte in "The Mourning Bride," with Mossop as Osmyn, when he made his last appearance at Drury Lane; on May 30th, she appeared as Edging in "The Careless Husband," and as Lucy in "The Old Man taught Wisdom;" on May 31st, she performed Lucy in "The Guardian," and on June 4th, she took the part of Inis in "The Wonder."

On the 19th of June, the "Beggar's Opera" was performed for the benefit of some distressed actors, in which Beard played Macheath; Miss Macklin, Polly, and Miss Barton, Lucy.   The following morning the *Public Advertiser* announced "The weather proving so unfavorable for plays, the benefit for the distressed actors, last night, did not answer so well as was expected, therefore, by particular desire, another play will be performed June 26, and several of the actors now in town have generously offered their assistance."

On the 19th of July was announced, for one night only, "Arden of Feversham," in which Miss Barton played the part of Maria.   This play was written by Lillo—it is only an alteration of an old play of the same name which was printed in 1592, and reprinted in 1770—to the later edition is prefixed an historical account of the murder of Arden, which took place on the 15th of February, 1550—in the play Arden is said to have obtained from the Duke of Somerset, at that time Protector, all the lands of the Abbey of Feversham—Greene, who had some claim on these lands, becomes his inveterate enemy—Ales, Arden's wife, is in love with Mosbie—Arden suspects her of an improper attachment to Mosbie, but has no absolute proof of it—Ales puts poison in her husband's broth—he dislikes the taste of it, and does not eat it—Arden goes to London with his friend Franklin—Greene hires two desperate ruffians, called Blacke Will and Shakebagge, to murder Arden—Michael has sworn to Ales that he would kill his master—he promises Blacke Will and Shakebagge to leave the door of the house unlocked, but, when it comes to the point, he is frightened and they are disappointed—they resolve to kill Arden on his journey from London—just as they are going to effect their purpose, Lord Chesny enters with his attendants, and Arden arrives in safety at Feversham—he is at last murdered in his own house—the murderers carry his body behind the Abbey and leave it there—the track of their feet is seen in the snow; so as to make it plain that Arden was not murdered where he was found, but carried thither after he was dead, blood is likewise discovered on the floor—Ales, Mosbie, Greene, and all the other persons, who were principals or abettors in the murder, are punished as they deserved. (Genest.)

Miss Barton's next appearance at Drury Lane was on the 25th of September, 1759, as Dorcas in "Romeo and Juliet." The announcement of her name, however, was now somewhat different owing to an important change in her circumstances; she was no longer Miss Barton but Mrs. Abington, late Miss Barton; under this name we shall, therefore, hereafter speak of her.

At this theatre, (Drury Lane) her engagements appear to have been very irregular for some time, during the first season she had, with the exception of playing Lucy, in "The Virgin Unmasked" and a new part in "The Minor," little or nothing to do, and things were not much better the second season. The theatre was, at this time, overstocked with popular female actresses, and advancement was extremely difficult, everything was monopolised by Mrs. and Miss Pritchard, Mrs.. Clive and Miss Macklin, whose popularity demanded the constant assignment to them of all the best characters. Miss Barton's salary was, in consequence, very moderate, being but thirty shillings a week, but even out of so limited an income she not only contrived to live but also to pay masters for instruction in various branches of the knowledge she was so deficient in, and which she sorely felt her need of. One of these masters was Mr. James Abington, a trumpeter, in the royal service, him she employed to teach her music, and afterwards married. In September, 1759, as we have said, she was announced as Mrs. Abington, a name she was destined afterwards to cover with lustre, but a name, so far as she was concerned, connected only with difficulty and unhappiness.

The rest of her appearances on the London Stage, after her marriage, were as Cherry, in the "Stratagem," on September 27th, as Lucinda, in the "Conscious Lovers," on October 2nd, as Lucetta, in the "Suspicious Husband," on October 5th, as Miss Lucy, in the "Old Man taught Wisdom," on October 6th, as Wishwell, in the "Double Gallant," on October 11th, as Foible, in the "Way of the World," on October 16th, as Melissa, in the "Lying Valet," on October 19th, and in some character not now ascertainable, on October 31st, in "High Life Below

Stairs." Genest says, "Mrs. Bradshaw and Mrs. Abington's
names are in the bill; Mrs. Bradshaw was the cook; Mrs.
Abington must have been Lady Bab or Lady Charlotte—her
name is not in the farce as printed; but if the Manuscript bill
had given us the names of all the female performers, it would
have been easy to have ascertained which of the two characters
she acted.

As Mrs. Abington grew popular, her husband showed unmis-
takeable signs of jealousy, whether justifiable or not it is not
easy to say, but things came to such a pitch, and the dissatisfac-
tion grew so mutual that by common consent they parted. A
regular agreement, was some time after entered into, and she
covenanted to pay him a certain sum per annum, on condition
that he neither came near her nor in any way molested her.
That he lived some years in the receipt of this pension is pretty
generally believed, but he soon disappeared from public notice,
and was speedily forgotten.

Owing to the great success which attended Mrs. Abington,
and the vociferous applause that ever greeted her appearance,
numerous enemies sprang up amongst other members of the
profession, who contrived often to make her position very un-
comfortable. The extraordinary jealousy that prevailed between
stage heroes and heroines, is not to be imagined by those who
never took a peep behind the curtain. If a new actor or actress
came on in the same walk as another who was supposed to have
established a reputation for that cast of parts, every invective
was called into play to diminish the merit and destroy the
reputation of the young performer. Mrs. Clive, who considered
Mrs. Abington as her professed rival in many capital characters,
could not refrain, upon every occasion, testifying the mortification she felt, and her severities were sometimes of the grossest
kind.

Five years after, upon Mrs. A——'s return to England, and
when again engaged by Garrick and meeting with the same
rapturous applause from the public, the same jealousy again
broke out and would sometimes display itself in bickerings and
altercations that were not entirely congenial to the delicacy of
the sex.

CHAPTER II.

Proposals from an Irish Manager—Garrick's indifference to her claims
and merits—Distressed state of the Irish Stage—Brown's struggles at
Smock-alley Theatre—Engagement of Mrs. Abington—Notes on the
History of the Irish Stage—Poor Pay of Actors, their sufferings—Re-
opening of Smock-alley Theatre—Mrs. Abington in The Stratagem—
Rapid increase of popularity—Arrival of Wilkinson—Mrs. Abington a
leader of fashion—Great success of High Life Below Stairs—Merchant of
Venice—Crow-street opposition to Smock-alley—Woodward and his
attempts to lower Mrs. Abington in public estimation, his failure—Mrs.
A. at Crow-street—Venice Preserved—The Lady's Last Stake—Way to
Keep Him—Suicidal Policy of the two Theatres, mutual loss—The Cork
Theatre—Further opposition between Smock-alley and Crow-street,
gradual decline of both—O'Keefe on Mrs. Abington's manner and style
of acting—Boaden on Mrs. A.—Wilkinson's retrospect.

We now come to a new phase of experience, altogether, in the
life of this popular actress. As we have seen, her engagements
on the London stage were neither sufficiently regular nor
remunerative to enable her to live with any degree of comfort
and happiness, it is not to be wondered at, therefore, that she
readily lent an ear to proposals which came from the managers
of other theatres, and, closing her engagements at Drury Lane,
proceeded to exercise her abilities in the Irish capital. Wilkinson says, " Mr. Garrick, not perceiving her merit, or in fear that
encouragement would be for claiming advancement of terms, did
not seem inclined to introduce her to advantage before the
public, but, my then intimate friend, Mrs. Abington formed a
better opinion of her own deserts, and, thinking Mr. Garrick
intended injury, instead of acting friendly, she, without ceremony,
suddenly eloped, in December, to her former manager and
acquaintance, Mr. Brown."

The Irish theatre at this time was in a most lamentable
condition, failure upon failure had attended every effort to
secure a return of prosperity, and put into the manager's hands
the means wherewith to discharge the arrears of salary due to
the actors. Disappointment after disappointment continually
occurred, and Victor was at last compelled to put Sheridan's
orders into execution, which were to dissolve the company from
acting any longer on his account, and to close the season—this
was done the 20th of April; at the same time, as the whole

Company were sufferers by arrears of salary, he offered them, from Sheridan, the use of the theatre if they chose to act some few more plays on their own account; this offer they accepted, but, not finding it answer, they finally closed the theatre May 28th.

"Victor distributed the money in his hands among the tradesmen, who had not received a farthing that season, and some of the poorer performers; this gave great offence to others, but he seems to have acted as uprightly as he could under the existing circumstances; he left Ireland at the close of the season, and here his account of the Irish stage ends."

"As Victor had returned to England, the distressed and scattered remains of the company were without a leader—every eye was turned to Brown—his indolence and inattention to business made him ill qualified for the office of manager, but his reputation as an actor and knowledge of the stage seemed to balance these defects, and almost every performer enlisted under him—on his part his affairs were desperate, he had nothing to lose, and if fortune smiled, he might reap some temporary advantage—he accordingly hired the theatre (Smock-alley) on moderate terms."

Hitchcock says "Innumerable were the difficulties Mr. Brown and the performers under his management had to struggle with —poverty, want of numbers, want of credit, a deserted ruinous theatre, contrasted to every advantage which power, success, strength of forces, universal favour and full coffers could confer. From circumstances the least expected, frequently arise events the most splendid. The disagreeable predicament in which Mr. Brown was placed proved the means of introducing to the world talents which have since excited its constant admiration. I mean no less than those of the famous Mrs. Abington. This lady was at that time very young. We are told that she played a few parts at Bath, when Mr. Brown was manager; also at Richmond, and in a few chance plays with Theophilus Cibber, in the Haymarket, and though she had at every opportunity, given specimens of those comic powers which were afterwards so amply displayed, yet it could scarcely have been supposed that in so short a time she would have been acknowledged the first comic actress on the stage. She had been at Drury Lane with Mr. Garrick, but judging from every appearance, that at that time, she would not have in London so favourable a field for the display of her abilities as Dublin presented, she listened to the proposals of Mr. Brown, who was then in town on the recruiting service."

Mr. Brown, indeed, the moment things were far enough arranged with regard to the hire of the theatre, communicated with Mrs. Abington, and so high was his opinion of her merit, that, without qualification, he offered her the choice of every leading character whatever, if she would quit her engagement at Drury Lane and join him in his venture. His offers were too tempting to an actress whose subordinate position rendered impossible a full development of her talents and who was in the receipt of but thirty shillings a week, to be refused, she accepted his proposals and embarked for Ireland, where she arrived early in December.

Particulars for a history of the Irish Stage are by no means plentiful, but it will be interesting just here to give a few of such as do exist, to shew the sphere of labour upon which the heroine of this memoir was entering.

Hitchcock, in his "Historical View," says "Having professedly confined myself to the rise and progress of the stage in this kingdom (Ireland), I shall decline entering into the minutiæ of its origin in Greece, or its first introduction into Rome, Britain or other countries; such disquisitions would be foreign to my present purpose; most of these points are besides sufficiently known, and nearly all have been already ably treated on. But whilst I endeavour to avoid everything superfluous or unnecessary, I find myself obliged to confess that my subject, at least the earlier part of it, does not, by its fruitfulness, sufficiently compensate for this exclusion. The era on which I am about to enter, like the remote parts of all history, is not of a nature the most productive or entertaining: the information to be attained is but very little, and even that little so enveloped in the prevailing ignorance and uncertainty of the times, that it affords but trifling materials for a clear or connected detail; even where accounts are most authentic, the remoteness of the periods prevents them from being, in any high degree, enlivened or interesting. At what period theatrical amusements first obtained footing in this kingdom has never yet been accurately ascertained; the general opinion is, that the drama arose later in this than in most countries of Europe. It was the unfortunate lot of the stage in this country, that its introduction and earlier progress were attended with more than usual uncertainty. The sister kingdom, can, with the greatest accuracy, trace the advances of her drama, step by step among them, from the conquest to the present times; but those advantages are denied us. The period generally agreed upon for its first introduction into this kingdom is the early part of the reign of Queen Elizabeth.

But an abstract from the annals of this city, mentions the performance of some plays in Henry the Eighth's time, before the Earl of Ossory, then Lord Lieutenant, and several of the nobility in Hoggin-green, now called College-green. We find little relative to the stage till the year 1635, the tenth of King Charles 1st when the first theatre in Dublin was raised. It was built in Werburgh-street, and established by John Ogilby, Esq., who was then historiographer to his majesty, and master of the revels under the Earl of Stafford, Lord Lieutenant of the kingdom.

The fair beginning of the Irish theatre, and seemingly prosperous advance of the stage, received, a short time after, a severe blow. "Langartha" was the last play that was acted at Werburgh-street theatre. The rebellion breaking out in the October of the same year, 1641, involved the whole kingdom in confusion. The drama naturally shared the fate of the state, with which it was so intimately connected. The theatre was shut up by order of the lords justices, and never afterwards opened. What became of the performers we cannot learn; perhaps, like some of their brethren in London, on a similar occasion, they entered into the service of their king and country. Of the manager, Mr. Ogilby, we are told that, exhausted and reduced by various misfortunes, he returned to England, where he intended to remain till the tumults should subside, and a happier revolution of affairs afford him an opportunity of resuming his former situation with safety and satisfaction. A period of twenty years elapsed before this wished-for change took place. At length, however, the nation having wearied itself out by intestine commotions, and, Charles the Second being happily placed on the throne, things began to recover an appearance of tranquility. At this time Mr. Ogilby's friends procured him a renewal of the patent from his majesty, and, in 1662, he returned to this kingdom to the particular joy of his own acquaintance, and the satisfaction of the public in general. Compassion for his sufferings, and a reviving taste for the drama, in a short time operated with such force as to influence the nobility and gentry to subscribe towards the building of a new theatre. Smock-alley, then called Orange-street, was the spot fixed on: a place, by its central situation, peculiarly adapted for such a purpose. The foundation was quickly laid, and the work advanced with such rapidity as to be ready for representations in the same year, 1662.

If we may be allowed to form an idea of the elegance of this theatre from its expense, we must imagine it to have been very considerable, as it is said to have cost upwards of two thousand pounds, a great sum at that time. In all probability, Smock-alley theatre was superior to those then in London, the haste, however, with which it was raised, was shortly after nearly proving fatal to it; for in the year 1671, during the representation, part of it fell down, by which accident two were killed and many severely wounded. This misfortune put another total stop to dramatic entertainments for a long time."

The name of this street, Smock-alley, took its appellation from Mother Bungy, of infamous memory, and was, in her time, a sink of debauchery, but a man being found murdered there, the miserable houses which then occupied that spot, were pulled down and handsome ones were afterwards built in their room, yet, though the place was thus purged of its infamy, it still retained its old name.

"The death of Mr. Ogilby proved the fore-runner of a long interval of inaction to the stage. New troubles arising and fresh tumults breaking forth, prevented its restoration. The unsettled state of the kingdom during the second James's reign, kept the public mind in too continued a state of alarm and apprehension to admit of any calm or peaceable relaxation. The people will necessarily attend to the preservation of their safety before they give way to the gratification of pleasure. It was, besides, peculiarly the fate of this kingdom to bear a conspicuous part in the prevailing disturbances, and be the melancholy scene of action for most of the events which ensued. Thus situated, every refined and rational entertainment was crushed and suppressed by the hand of violence. For these reasons, the re-establishment of the theatre did not take place till the revolution had once more restored tranquility and presented a prospect of peace with her smiling train returning to bless this divided kingdom with her permanent abode."

Of the years intervening—between this early period and the time of Mrs. Abington's appearance, it would be out of place here to offer more than a brief and passing word; suffice it to say that vicissitudes and trials of all and every kind, accompanied with occasional gleams of sunshine, were the lot of the Irish Stage. Again and again, owing to national troubles, to severe weather, and to the poverty of the people, were the performances suspended. For the paltry pay offered most of the actors, a greater part of which they never got, it is wonderful that men and women could be found willing to go through the hard work and submit to the tyranny and caprice of the public, incidental to the profession. Yet every now and then, actors and actresses from London, such as Quin, Mrs. Woffington,

B

Wilkes, Mrs. Clive, Mrs. Cibber and Sheridan made their appearance, and plays were got up and performed in the best of styles. Genest says, "It is scarcely credible, though strictly true, that before Sheridan's time, Isaac Sparks had but twelve shillings per week—Dyer, eight—Elrington, a guinea, and the rest in proportion,—miserable as these pittances were, they many weeks received not above half their respective demands— perhaps the following anecdote, though from unquestionable authority, will hardly be believed—the acting managers as they were called, were so reduced in their finances and exhausted in their credit, that they were once obliged to repair to the theatre on the evening of a play dinnerless—the first shilling that came into the house they despatched for a loin of mutton—the second for bread—the third for liquor, and so on till they had satisfied the demands of nature."

Under such adverse circumstances it is a wonder that despair did not overwhelm everybody, and the profession die out altogether; the love of the actor for his art, however, survived through long and dreary seasons of privation and suffering, and was ultimately rewarded for its constancy by the dawn of more prosperous times.

Mr. Brown, having completed his arrangements in London, and secured the services of Mrs. Abington, returned at once to Dublin, and exerted himself to the utmost in the preparation of his theatre for the coming season. His finances were at a very low ebb indeed, but he endeavoured to use them to the best advantage in the repair and decoration of the building in Smock-alley, and so far succeeded in rendering it presentable, that he was able to open it on Friday, the 11th of December, 1759, with the "Stratagem," when Mrs. Abington, as Mrs. Sullen, made her first appearance on the Irish stage; Brown, himself, playing Archer, and Waker, Scrub. "On this occasion Brown spoke a prologue, written by himself, entreating the favour and protection of the town. Every effort which could be used was tried to procure a respectable audience for the first night, and the curiosity generally prevalent on such occasions induced many to visit their long-favoured scene of amusement. The company was altogether tolerably liked, and hope animated their endeavours. Their next essay was on the Wednesday following, when Mr. Brown appeared in his favourite Benedict, which, with Mrs. Abington's Beatrice, were as truly capital pieces of acting as ever were presented to the public."

"As Mr. Brown was acknowledged to be equal to any comedian living in such characters as Brass in the "Confederacy," Bayes in the "Rehearsal," Ranger in the "Suspicious Husband," Sir John Brute, Felix, Roebuck, Marplot, Dr. Wolf in the "Non Juror," "Don John in the "Chances," Monsieur Le Medicin, Lord Chalkstone, Aspin, Abel Drugger; so did Mrs. Abington surpass the most sanguine expectations in Corinna, Clarinda, Flora, and Violante, Lady Fanciful, &c. Each night she appeared she added to her reputation, and before the season closed, notwithstanding every disadvantage, and many these were, particularly that of not having received the London stamp of fashion and approbation, she was considered as one of the first and most promising actresses on the stage."

"In the embarrassed state of the Smock-alley Company, fortune raised an unexpected relief. This was the arrival of Mr. Wilkinson in Ireland, and his almost immediate engagement with Mr. Brown. He proved to be a very seasonable and necessary reinforcement. He had great connections in Dublin, and general opinion gave him the preference to Mr. Foote. His terms were, shares above twenty pounds, and a clear benefit. The former proved of little emolument; the latter, highly productive. He appeared on Friday, January 4th, 1760, after the comedy of "Much ado about Nothing," in a piece of Mr. Foote's never at that time acted in Ireland, called the "Diversions of the Morning." He was well supported and received much applause. His imitation of his late friend Mr. Foote was highly relished, and he repeated it on the Monday following, after Brown's Shylock and Mrs. Abington's Portia, to about forty pounds! (Hitchcock.)

Mrs. Abington's acting, especially in certain pieces, fairly took the town by storm, and her taste in dress was regarded by the ladies of fashion as so good and correct that it became quite the rage to wear articles bearing her name. Her position was very different to what it had been when employed at Drury Lane, leading instead of subordinate and inferior parts were now assigned to her, and the improvement in her earnings enabled her to make the arrangement alluded to, by which she relieved herself of the presence of her uncongenial husband.

The farce of "High Life below Stairs" seems to have been one of the pieces in which she was particularly successful. Hitchcock says, "Here I must notice the extraordinary success of the farce of "High Life below Stairs." It would exceed the limits prescribed to this work to copy at full length the circumstances attending this piece, which Mr. Wilkinson so agreeably describes, suffice it to say that this pleasing farce had escaped the notice of the Crow-street managers. In the multiplicity of their business, engrossed as they were in the preparation of grand tragedies and pantomimes, they probably might not have thought it worthy of their attention. Mr. Wilkinson luckily fixed upon it. He communicated his intentions to Mrs. Abington who not only approved of his choice, but consented to play the part of Kitty. The piece had been brought out at Drury Lane, so early as the month of October, where it had met with the greatest success. They had both frequently seen it before they left London, and were therefore quite perfect in the stage business proper to it. It lay within the compass of the company; could be got up at a very little expense, and no comparison could be drawn to their disadvantage."

In allusion to this, Tate Wilkinson says, "Mrs. Abington approved of my thought for that farce, and she not only consented but seemed pleased with Mrs. Kitty; and, though she had played several leading characters, yet our receipts only ran from £20 to £25, and at best £40, in general, one night with the other. She laboured under great disadvantages, and such as much repelled her endeavours to get admittance in the court of fame, for though she was much approved, yet, as she had not then a London stamp, and as Mrs. Dancer was firmly established in Dublin, her merit was much forgot when her guests were departed."

Hitchcock proceeds "Mr. Wilkinson tells us Mr. Ryder's Sir Harry was a very excellent piece of acting, and helped the piece materially. A Mr. Gates, a very conceited actor, played Lord Duke. His faults and oddities served but to heighten the extravagance of the character. Mr. Heaton's Philip was as well as such a part could be. He was a very good actor in all the dry clowns, clodpoles, &c. Miss Phillips, (aunt to the present Mrs. Jordan) who was also of a conceited turn though sensible and well educated, made the part of Lady Bab better than any other actress I ever saw attempt it; myself from observation and youth must have been stupid, not to have made a very good Jemmy, the Country Boy, and, as the great personage always appears last in triumphant entries and processions, so in Mrs. Kitty, Mrs. Abington advanced. The whole circle were in surprise and rapture, each asking the other how such a treasure could have possibly been in Dublin, and almost in a state of obscurity; such a jewel was invaluable, and their own tastes and judgments they feared would justly be called in question, if this daughter of Thalia was not immediately taken by the hand, and distinguished as her certain and striking merit demanded. To this I shall only add, that so successful were they in their representation of this farce that it was repeated upwards of a dozen times during the remaining part of the season."

On the 7th of January, 1760, was acted the " Merchant of Venice," Shylock by Brown ; Portia by Mrs. Abington, with "Diversions of the Morning," Lady Pentweazel, Wilkinson. Genest says " Wilkinson did not take off any of the regular performers at C. S. as he did not wish to affront Barry, but contented himself with imitating Foote, who was then at Dublin. Barry and Mossop, in consequence, took tickets of him at his benefit—Wilkinson acted Lear—Mrs. Amlet to Brown's Brass, and Mrs. Abington's Corinna—Cadwallader to her Becky— Lord Chalkstone and Old Man in " Lethe " to her Frenchman, which she played with great applause.

" His (Wilkinson's) benefit was February 15th, when notwithstanding there was a deep snow, and a very strong play at Crow Street, the house overflowed in every part, for Wilkinson had many friends in Dublin—the receipt was £172, the greatest ever known at that time in that theatre—Douglas was the play ; Norval, Wilkinson ; Lady Randolph, Mrs. Ibbott ; with Tea, and (never acted in Ireland) High Life Below Stairs. Lovel, Wilkinson ; Sir Harry, Ryder ; Duke, Yates ; Philip, Heaton ; Kitty, Mrs. Abington. In consequence of the overflow of this evening, another night was demanded for the outstanding tickets, this was fixed for February 21st, when there was £150 in the house, though £40 or less seem to have been the average receipt one night with another—the play was "The Orphan of China "— Zamti, Wilkinson (which character he says himself he had acted before and been well received in) ; Mandane, Mrs. Ibbott—with High Life again."

The Crow-street manager advertised against it that they had dresses preparing in London, which were to be sent over, and intimating Mr. Murphy, the author, would follow to see it rehearsed," to which Mr. Brown replied, in the following paragraph :

" ' The Orphan of China ' being a tragedy not in anyway difficult or mysterious to those who do not require to be parrotted in their parts, we can assure the public that it is now in perfect readiness, and will be performed this evening at the theatre, in Smock-alley, without the assistance of the author : for as plays are sometimes revived long after the author's decease, what would become of them in a theatre when it is found essentially necessary for the poet to attend the latter rehearsals ? And as to the dresses, neither the Chinese or

Tartar are absolutely unknown in Ireland, therefore, it is hoped, it will not be objected as a fault that we have not gone to London either for design or materials."

Mandane was acted by Mrs. Ibbott, a lady of merit in speaking blank verse. There was £150 in the house the second night of "High Life," and it went off, if possible, with more *eclat* than on the first representation, and Abington resounded in all parts of the theatre. I remember the second night of "High Life." Mrs. Abington said to me (with great propriety), "Good G——, Mr. Wilkinson! what could provoke you to blunder so? why should you think of a tragedy, when you had reason to expect so fine a house, as the company are not equal to the performance?" Certainly, her being so noticed in Kitty would, in speculation have been materially bettered with that lady in a leading character in comedy; the house would have felt much injured and diminished in profit had half price been taken, but it neither was then, nor ever since has been, the custom to take under price in Dublin.—I had a strong party made again by my friends, which, with Mrs. Abington's name, settled the business to my advantage; but I told her my reason for taking a tragedy was solely that its gravity might aid and give spirit when the new farce came on. The truth was, I wanted to entertain myself with acting Mr. Garrick's part of the Chinese Zamti, in which I was so fortunate as actually to please beyond mediocrity, though dressed in an old red damask bed gown, which was what we termed the stock bed gown for Brabantino and many other parts and had for time immemorial been of that venerable use, and bore the marks of many years' faithful servitude.

I was certainly lucky in my two nights answering with such swimming success, and more fortunate still, when I inform the reader, twenty-four hours after would have given the last night a severe blow, and greatly prejudiced it, for the next day not only an alarm was received, but several expresses arrived, that Thurot had actually landed at Carrickfergus. This, of course, caused the army to march by beat of drum instantly, to give immediate assistance and repel the invaders, and it naturally occasioned a general panic and confusion and was the topic of universal conversation throughout the city of Dublin, even the Abington that day was not mentioned. It quickly subsided, and Mons. Thurot made an unfortunate retreat, as stands on well known record.

"High Life Below Stairs" was perpetually acted and with never failing success. In ten days after its being performed, Abington's cap was so much the taste with the ladies of fashion and ton, that there was not a milliner's shop window, great or small, but was adorned with it, and in large letters ABINGTON appeared to attract the passer by. This Abington-rage Woodward endeavoured to suppress by ridicule, not here fit to be described, but all too little, or rather to no purpose, for her reputation as an actress daily increased, though on the remote ground of an unfashionable ill supported theatre. (Wilkinson.)

This "Henry Woodward was born in the borough of Southwark, in the year 1717, where his father had for some time followed the business of a tallow chandler, for which profession the son was intended. Very fortunately, however, for the youth, he was placed in Merchant Taylor's School, a seminary long remarkable for the men of genius it has produced in various professions. There Harry made a rapid progress, and acquired a taste for the classics which in the future part of his life, he frequently displayed to the surprise of such of his company as had not been acquainted with the manner in which he was educated. A circumstance happened when he was about fourteen years of age which gave him a strong bias in favour of a theatrical life, it was briefly this:—From the uncommon run of the "Beggar's Opera," Mr. Rich who was at that time manager of the Theatre Royal, in Lincoln's-Inn-Fields, was encouraged to represent it by children. In this lilliputian company Harry performed the part of Peachum with great success; and having thus entertained a passion for the drama, could never afterwards divest himself of it. He had begun with the lowest of pantomimical characters, and went on in regular succession from a frog to a hedgehog, an ape and a bear, till he arrived at the summit of his ambition, harlequin. His talents at this period produced him a genteel salary at Covent-Garden Theatre, and in consequence of the death of Chapman, the comedian, he had an opportunity of exhibiting his comic powers in their full force. Marplot, Lord Foppington, Sir Andrew, Aguecheck, Touchstone, Captain Parolles, &c., were all represented by him with an uncommon degree of applause.

In the year 1747, Mr. Sheridan, manager of Smock Alley Theatre, Dublin, engaged him at no less a sum than five hundred pounds to perform the ensuing winter. In this engagement Mr. Woodward was articled as a comedian and harlequin, in both which departments he was extremely useful, and brought great receipts. In the former character he attacked Mr. Foote in his favourite piece of "Tea, or the Diversions of the Morning," with such superior strength of humour, ridicule and mimicry, as beat him out of the field; and in the latter, got up

a new pantomime (since altered to " Queen Mab ") which did
his invention great credit and his employer considerable service.
As a comedian he was unequalled in his cast of parts, as a com-
poser of pantomimes he had infinite merit, his merit likewise
as a principal actor in those amusements, was considerable.
(Thespian Dictionary.)

Whatever Woodward's power and influence over other actors
might be, he altogether failed, as we have said, in his attempt
to lessen the fame acquired by Mrs. Abington, on the contrary,
that fame increased every day and Hitchcock says " she became
an object for the Crow-street managers to fix their attention
upon, many persons of the first rank earnestly interested
themselves in her favour, and wished much to see their new
favourite transplanted to the genial sunshine of the Royal
Theatre before the close of the present season, and they exerted
themselves so strenuously that an engagement was soon concluded, she was to perform for a few nights for a clear benefit.

Her first appearance at Crow-street was on the 22nd of May,
1760, in the character of Lady Townley, and Lucinda in the
Englishman in Paris, and so generally was she patronised that
part of the pit was laid into the boxes and there was a great
overflow from every part of the house."

The theatre closed June 9th with Oroonoko, with the Virgin
Unmasked, by Mrs. Abington.

" Woodward immediately set off for London to provide for
the next season—he was followed in some few weeks by Mossop,
on similar business. Thus ended one of the most brilliant seasons
ever known in Ireland, at the end of which, Barry and Woodward found themselves greatly deficient, and this deficiency
increased every year, till it involved them in total ruin. So heavy
and numerous a company had never been collected—the weekly
payments to performers alone often amounted to £170—tradesmen's bills, and servants' salaries frequently were not less
than £200 more—the receipts of the theatre were not equal
to these expenses, and the managers, who had launched into
such extravagance, felt too late the consequences of their im-
prudence. Whether the interests of the dramatic world and the
public in general would be best served by one or by two theatres
had been much disputed, but it appears clear as a matter of
fact, that Dublin could not maintain two play-houses without
ruin to one or both parties." (Hitchcock.)

The Crow-street theatre re-opened in the autumn, and on the
17th of November, Mrs. Abington played the part of Lucy
in the " Beggar's Opera."

"As soon as the managers found they were to be opposed by Mossop, they offered her an eligible engagement, which she thought proper to accept—rightly judging that her abilities would receive greater support and have better opportunities of displaying themselves with Woodward than with Mossop— it was indeed no easy task to adjust the distribution of parts between her and Mrs. Dancer, however it was agreed to divide them as near as possible with impartiality." (Hitchcock.)

This was followed soon after by "Venice Preserved" with first time, Queen Mab—Harlequin, Woodward; Columbine, Mrs. Abington, and then

"The Lady's Last Stake"—Lord George Brilliant, Woodward : Mrs. Conquest, Mrs. Dancer: Miss Notable, Mrs. Abington : who in girlish characters was at this time superior to any actress from her naïveté and genuine traits of nature—she acted Miss Prue to Mrs. Dancer's Anglica, and did herself infinite credit in Polly Honeycombe.

In February 1761, was acted for the first time in Ireland, "The way to Keep Him," when Mrs. Abington is said to have added greatly to her reputation by the easy, elegant, finished portrait of the woman of fashion which she exhibited in the Widow Belmour.

Crow-street theatre closed on the 9th of June with "Every Man in his Humour."

"The latter part of the season had proved a continued disagreeable scene of exertions and rivalship, productive of infinite trouble, great expense, and vexation, attended with loss of reputation and very little profit, and gradually involving the managers of each house in that ruin which finally overtook both. It seemed to be laid down as a rule by the respective managers, that no sooner was a piece announced to be in rehearsal or for exhibition by the one, than the other strained every nerve, no matter with what propriety to prepossess the public with an idea of its being preparing in a superior style by him, or boldly advertising the very piece, on the same evening, sometimes without an idea of its being performed, but merely to divide or suspend the general curiosity. Thus the little ballad farce of the Lottery, which, from the limited number of after-pieces, more than its intrinsic merit, was then much in fashion, was no sooner exhibited at Smock-alley, than the week following presented it to the public at Crow-street; supported by the Jack Stocks of Mr. Griffith, and the admirable Chloe of Mrs. Abington.

"The Wife's Resentment," revived at the theatre Royal, with Mr. Woodward, Mrs. Dancer, and Mrs. Abington, immediately produced an advertisement announcing the same play with Mr. Mossop, though he had not the least idea of exhibiting it.

Mr. Colman's farce of Polly Honeycombe, then performing with great eclat at Drury-lane, was, in like manner advertised by both parties, but only produced at Crow-street, on which occasion, as before noticed, Mrs. Abington acquired infinite credit in the part of Polly.

But the greatest piece of generalship manifested through the whole of this doubtful contest was respecting the new tragedy of "The Orphan of China," written by Arthur Murphy, Esq., and at that time exhibiting with uncommon reputation in London. The great fame and popularity of this piece, rendered it an obect of peculiar attention to both houses in Dublin ; but to attain their object they pursued quite different lines of conduct. The play being printed, was consequently in possession of both. Mr. Mossop observed a discreet silence on the subject, and kept his designs as much a secret as possible. The managers of Crow-street on the contrary, confident of their strength, but rather injudiciously I should think, for several weeks, made a great parade of their intentions of producing it with a pomp and magnificence, equal to that of Drury-lane ; informing the public of the extraordinary expense they were at, in having all the dresses made in London, from models imported from China, and an entire new set of scenes painted for the occasion, in the true Chinese style, by the celebrated Carver, then deservedly in the highest reputation.

When the expectations of the town were raised to the utmost pitch, and curiosity strained to the highest point without the least previous hint dropped, most unexpectedly, early on Monday Morning, January 5th, 1761, bills were posted up, announcing the representation of this much talked of tragedy that very evening, at Smock-alley Theatre. The scenery, dresses, and decorations entirely new, with this specious and popular addition, the characters will be all new dressed in the manufactures of this kingdom.

The truth was, they had bespoke dresses, to be made in London, on the models of the Drury-lane habits, but had not the least expectation of their arriving in time. As they knew that everything depended on their producing it before the other house, certain they had not an equal chance on equal terms, the dresses and scenery of Crow-street being so much superior, they used evey exertion possible. The tragedy was rehearsed three times a day, and Mr. Tracey, then tailor to the theatre, working day and night on the dresses, they were completed in eight and forty hours. The event proved they acted right. The Orphan of China drew five tolerable houses to Smock-alley, before they were able to get it out at Crow-street, and then it did not answer the expense they had been at. The dresses and scenery were truly characteristic, but the curiosity of the public had been in a great measure previously gratified. (Hitchcock.)

In the summer of 1761, the Crow-street managers opened a new theatre at Cork.

" During the infancy of the stage in Ireland, Cork was frequently visited by itinerant companies of comedians, who sometimes spent an entire winter there with much emolument. The theatres on these occasions were generally temporary structures, hastily erected for the immediate purpose. In process of time, the Dublin managers extended their views to a city so capable of supplying the intervening time, between the close and the opening of their winter seasons. The country companies were obliged to give place to his majesty's servants, and a new theatre was erected at the corner of Princess-street, in George-street, and opened in the year 1736. Messrs. Barry and Woodward, with a judicious eye, beheld the many advantages likely to arise from a theatre on a more extended scale, in so capital a situation ; the present one being much too small for their processions, and pantomimes. They had accordingly advertised a subscription for raising a fund towards building a new theatre. The proposal was eagerly embraced; in a few weeks the money was raised. The ground was purchased in Georges-street, not far from the former buildings, in a situation which every day improved, and the work began. The model adopted was that of Crow-street ; the dimensions were nearly as large, except having but one gallery. It was finished and ready for the reception of the company this summer, and the public expressed great pleasure at so great an improvement in their favourite amusement." (Hitchcock.)

The theatre was duly opened with a company of unusual strength, and the season proved to be uncommonly brilliant and profitable. Shuter went with them to Cork, but Mrs. Abington remained in Dublin, to which city the company returned, flushed with success.

Mr. Woodward at once left for England for the purpose of endeavouring to make up for certain losses he had sustained in his company, and which, in the opinion of some, gave a preponderance of strength to Mr. Mossop. Pretty nearly equal in quality were the two companies, but Mrs. Abington and Mrs. Fitzhenry had been won over to Mr. Mossop, jealous of the

power of Mrs. Dancer, and Mr. Ryder too, who had been absent
for some time, returned to Smock-alley to take that lead which
his merit so highly entitled him to. The theatre opened in
October with the "Spanish Fryar."

"Among the ill effects produced by two rival theatres, one
was, that of seducing performers from their first-engagements.
Changing sides was so much the fashion, and some gentlemen
were so much in this mode of manœuvre, that they were sometimes led into great mistakes, and have often been called to
play at one theatre, when they have been found dressing at
another." (Hitchcock.)

At this time Mrs. Abington played Termagant.

"Wilkinson, who had arrived in January, and was engaged
for twelve nights, acted Lady Pentweazel—his benefit (February
22nd) was a very great one—"Jealous Wife" Oakly, Wilkinson;
Major Oakly, Baddeley; Lord Trinket, Jefferson; Charles, Reed;
Russet, Heaphy; Lady Freelove, Miss Kennedy; Harriet, Miss
Macartney; Mrs. Oakly, Mrs. Abington; with "Tea," Buck's
"Have at you all," and the farce of the "Country House."

After his engagement was over, Mrs. Abington requested him
to act for her benefit in an interlude, which proved a foolish business—the play was "Rule a Wife."   Lean, Mossop; Peres,
Brown; Estifania, Mrs. Abington. She spoke an Epilogue in
which there were some lines sarcastically aimed at Woodward,
who deserved this at her hands, for what he had said of her
about two years before; they were very severe, and as she
delivered them excellently in Woodward's manner, he was stung
to the quick. (Genest.)

The comedy of "All in the Wrong," written by Mr. Murphy,
was then performing with such *eclat* in London, as to make it
well worthy the attention of the Dublin managers. Each party
prepared for its representation. It was announced with much
pomp, as in rehearsal at Crow-street, when, after five or six days
hard study it was most unexpectedly, one morning, without any
previous notice, advertised for that evening at Smock-alley. The
consequence was it was pushed on six nights before they could
possibly bring it forward at Crow-street, and then it was not
worth much to either party. Notwithstanding which, it was
played sixteen nights that season at Smock-alley.

Notwithstanding any little temporary success, during the
course of the season, the interests of the Crow-street theatre
were visibly on the decline. The Lord Lieutenant, the Earl of
Halifax, it is true, afforded his patronage, and generally commanded at least once a week. Several very excellent pantomimes

also, particularly two new ones, the " Fair " and the "Sorcerer," were produced. Yet in spite of all these advantages and exertions, the managers found their receipts infinitely inferior to their disbursements, which indeed were too heavy for a Dublin theatre to support. The succeeding season, in Dublin, exhibited nothing remarkable. The theatres were visibly on the decline ; unable to support the expense of the prevailing opposition, the managers found every day added to the precariousness and danger of their situation, without the least prospect of relief. The receipts of the two theatres were scarcely sufficient to defray the expenditure of one. The greatest contention seemed to be, not who should gain most, but who should lose the least. Towards the end of the season Mr. Mossop produced Mrs. Abington, whose popularity rendered her at this time a welcome visitor, but who not being so well supported as she ought, had not, consequently so much attraction. Smock-alley closed much sooner than Crow-street. (Hitchcock.)

This brings Mrs. Abington's career in Dublin to a close, acting sometimes at Crow-street and at other times at Smock-alley, always with success, and winning the loudest applause and approbation, she thus passed five years of her life. Henceforward we shall have to speak of her appearances on the stage of the English metropolis.

In closing this section of our memoir, we shall give a few further specimens of the very high estimation in which she was held by those who were competent judges of her professional ability during her stay in Ireland.

O'Keefe says " her manner was most charmingly fascinating, and her speaking voice melodious. She had peculiar tricks in acting ; one was turning her wrist, and seeming to stick a pin in the side of her waist ; she was also very adroit in the use of her fan, and though equally capital in fine ladies and hoydens, was never seen in low or vulgar characters. On her benefit night the pit was always railed into the boxes. Her acting shone brightest when doing Estifania, with Brown's Copper Captain, Don Juan Benedict, Bayes, Sir John Restless, and Barnaby Brittle. At those times in Ireland, every comedy and comic opera ended with a country dance by the characters, which had a charming and most exhilarating effect, both to the dancer and lookers on. A particular tune when he danced, was called Brown's Rant ; in the course of the dance, as he and his partner advanced to the lamps at the front of the stage, he had a peculiar step, which he quaintly tipped off to advantage, and the audience always expecting this, repaid him with applause."

Boaden writes of her:—"Ireland as a school for a young
actress, had been long rendered of first-rate importance by the
brilliant career of Mrs. Abington, who acted at both the Dublin
theatres, and unquestionably possessed very peculiar and un-
approached talent. She, I think, took more entire possession
of the stage, than any actress I have ever seen, there was however, no assumption in her dignity; she was a lawful and
graceful sovereign, who exerted her full power, and enjoyed her
established prerogatives. The ladies of her day wore the hoop
and its concomitants. The spectator's exercise of the fan was
really no play of fancy. Shall I say that I have never seen it
in a hand so dexterous as that of Mrs. Abington. She was a
woman of great application, to speak as she did, required more
thought than usually attends female study. For the greater
part of the sex rely upon an intention which seldom misleads
them, such discernment as it gives becomes habitual, and is
commonly sufficient, or sufficient for common purposes. But
common-place was not the station of Abington. She was always
beyond the surface, untwisted all the chains which bind ideas
together, and seized upon the exact cadence and emphasis by
which the point of the dialogue is enforced. Her voice was of
a high pitch and not very powerful. Her management of it
alone made it an organ, yet this was so perfect that we sometimes converted the mere effect into a cause, and supposed it
was the sharpness of the tone that had conveyed the sting. Yet,
her figure considered, her voice rather sounded inadequate; its
articulation, however, gave both strength and smartness to it,
though it could not give sweetness. You heard her well, and
without difficulty, and it is the first duty of a public speaker to
be audible and intelligible. Her deportment is not so easily
described; more womanly than Farren, fuller, yet not heavy, like
Younge, and far beyond even the conception of modern fine
ladies. Mrs. Abington remains in memory as a thing for chance
to restore us, rather than design, and revive our polite comedy
at the same time."

"From dear Dublin and good friends,"writes Wilkinson, " I
took my farewell early in March, 1760, and left Mrs Abington
going on in full career to reach the pinnacle where she has many
years sat smiling, and been looked at and admired with sincere
pleasure and respect by the first persons in both the kingdoms."
At that juncture she had many disadvantages to struggle with,
such as the encountering Barry's, Woodward's, Mossop's,
Fitzhenry's, and Dancer's benefit nights at Crow-street, which
summonses the Dublin world obeyed; and Smock-alley, which

had sometimes by luck her attractions and chance benefits, &c., dragged on perforce, but in the ides of March was on the verge of a certain downfall. Plays were thus acted then in Crow-street. "The Orphan."—Castalia, Mr. Barry; Chamont, Mr. Mossop; Polydore, Mr. Dexter; Monimia, Mrs. Dancer; and all the other characters well dressed and supported, as may be supposed, by referring to the list of the company, with the advantage of new scenery, a new and elegant theatre, &c., "All for Love."—Marc Antony, Mr. Barry; Dolabella, Mr. Jefferson; Ventidius, Mr. Mossop; Octavia, Mrs. Dancer; Cleopatra, Mrs. Fitzhenry. "Alexander the Great," cast in the same manner. Comedies, with Woodward, Macklin, Mrs. Kennedy, Vernon, &c., with the persons just mentioned: so that take it all together, it was equal to any company I ever saw in London, and much better than I have frequently seen there, though the old house was sinking rapidly, had not Mrs. Abington by her strength of arm upheld it; yet it was indeed restored to its ancient dignity and family honours for one joyful, happy night of ecstacy, and that was no less than on the enjoyment of the Abington, at what might be truly called her own night.

A strange play for Mrs. Abington to choose it was! "A New Way to pay Old Debts," March 17th, but she made amends by other performances that evening, on which occasion the old, the young, the gay, all bowed at her shrine as the Temple of Thalia, such ascendancy had she thus quickly acquired over the public opinion. This attachment towards the latter end of the season did not cease with the million, for it is true, to attend the falling theatre was a great bore, yet, still languishing for Abington, and wishing to see her on a better cultivated and good promising soil, for her merit to be nourished and matured by a perpetual sunshine, a party of leading persons proposed her acting a few nights at Crow-street, before the theatrical campaign closed; gave assurance of patronage on her nights of performance, and on a clear night being promised and fixed for Mrs. Abington, in return for her support to the managers' nights, she complied with their desire.

Mrs. Abington had not any occasion to request this change of place or accumulation of honours, as they were not owing to solicitation on her part, but the persons of distinction were stimulated to this desire by their eagerness to satisfy themselves by seeing the new favourite transplanted amidst the gaudy flowers of Crow-street, where they did not doubt but she would soon gain a state of distinction whenever the artists of theatrical florists met to signalize, distinguish, and decide the claims to the prizes when they scrutinized on the play-house auriculas and the gaudy tulips.

All that was contracted for by the persons of quality for the managers and Mrs. Abington, was, I believe, strictly abided by, faithfully executed, and answered to the infinite satisfaction of all parties. The persons of lead and fashion were entertained and paid for their purchase of choice, not compulsion; the managers got money. Mrs. Abington had a surprising and magnificent audience at her benefit—so I can guess they were all pleased. Not that I would venture to pronounce all were entirely satisfied, for there never can be great commotion at the real court, or behind the theatrical curtain, but it must and will affect and hurt the minds of those concerned. A lord disappointed of his court expectation, seldom (I will not say never) rejoices at the preference given to another, so the actor or actress buoyed up with the pleasing tide of success, must be alarmed when he or she not only hears but feels the treading of the kibe by a courtier or new raised favourite.

It not only is galling, but more is really to be said for it than is always allowed. That merit should be cherished and raise its head, is a first principle and duty from the audience and the manager; but when considered as a lessening of pride and income to another, it is a serious matter to the soul so piqued, nor are any minds so soon hurt on the least frivolous occasions as those of the theatre; and sometimes it happens a phenomenon really starts up.—Mrs. Jordan, four years ago only, playing at York, at £1 11s. 6d. per week, was thought really very clever by London performers who saw her there, but all said it would not do among them, yet by great luck, great good fortune indeed, and to be for an hundred years at least remembered in theatrical annals, she in two years afterwards made even the London managers dread her frown, her non-compliance, her elopement, her toothache, or her phantom of horror which she has threatened them with, to the terror of tragedy itself, and made them comply with the most exhorbitant terms.—A happy lot indeed! A happy rise!—I hope it will last her life, and with care make her career successful as it has so providentially and wonderfully begun.

Mrs. Jordan is certainly the lucky child of fortune, but led, caressed, and nursed in the lap of nature; she is undoubtedly the reigning Thalia of the age 1790, and deservedly so; and to her comic talents, archness, whim and fancy, I submissively bow, and also acknowledge her humanity and goodness to her late parent, but am compelled as Mr. Manager, to declare, like Mr.

Foote in his "Devil upon Two Sticks," (as greatness knows itself) that Mrs. Jordan, at making a bargain, is too many for the cunningest devil of us all.

Speaking of Mrs. Abington's merit in the comic line occasioned my introducing Mrs. Jordan's name at the same time, and as I cannot yet quit Mrs. Abington's situation, whom I left at her great benefit in Dublin, it may be easily supposed from her being so happily transplanted, that she derived many advantages from playing with Mr. Woodward, Mr. Macklin, and other regulars; nor was Mr. Woodward a loser but a gainer by the acquisition to his stage, as Mrs. Abington rebounded the ball to the force with which Woodward struck it.

But now another irksome matter arose in consequence of her success; where our passions or partialities are predominant, it is not always reason can be listened to or obeyed. It was very apparent, from motives of policy and sound judgment that Mrs. Abington should be engaged on the most eligible terms, otherwise they could not hope such a rising actress would article. To this Woodward did not hesitate, as it assisted his comedies, and an agreement was settled for the following winter. But when it is considered Mrs. Dancer then played all the principal characters in comedy as well as in tragedy, it made the sea of Crow-street troubled; the waves that looked calm turned to rough breakers, and the open sea to rise and threaten a storm, for when those ladies acted in the same plays, as in the "Lady's Last Stake," Mrs. Dancer played Mrs. Conquest; Mrs. Abington, Miss Notable; (by the bye Mrs. Jordan, why have you neglected Miss Notable?) In "Love for Love," Angelica, Mrs. Dancer; Miss Prue, Mrs. Abington; and many other plays, where they were often mutually concerned, and sometimes where Mrs. Abington was the rival Fine Lady, which some plays admit where the parts are of equal consequence. Miss Notable and Miss Prue, from the archness and excellent acting of Mrs. Abington, seemed to have the decision at the winning post for fame, but I must observe, those comic characters will ever, when well supported, obtain the loudest applause, however well acted Mrs. Conquest and Angelica may be by any actress whatever, as the hoydens are so well calculated for what we term stage effect.

This division of hands from the upper and lower part of the house, it was not likely Mrs. Dancer (as queen of the theatre) could relish or gulp down by any means to make the Abington pleasing or agreeable. This proved and grew offensive to Mr. Barry, as he was then as passionate an inamorato as ever youthful poet fancied when he loved, and would have thrown immediate bars to the engagement with Mrs. Abington, and greatly

c

impeded her rapid good fortune, had not a sudden and important matter of astonishment at that time started up to the amazement of every faculty of eyes, ears, &c., for Barry and Woodward, lulled in their long wished for security, became the dupes of their own arts and made the wandering prodigal (Woodward) begin seriously to reflect, and severely repent his foolish conduct in leaving his enviable situation in London, and above all the horror of losing what he had saved with so much care. This dreadful alarm was no less than the certainty of a report being confirmed as real, which at first they treated as unlikely, vague and impossible, but it proved strictly true, that Mr. Mossop from the encouragement and instigation of all his friends, and patronised by the Countess of Brandon, of powerful sway, with many leaders of fashion, had certainly taken Smock-alley theatre on a long lease, purposing many expensive and gaudy alterations, &c., to oppose Crow-street, in the month of October, the ensuing season. Barry and Woodward (to prevent if possible the dreadful undertaking) made him liberal offers, nay, even humbled themselves before him, to entreat Mossop to name his own terms. All this only increased his pride, and he spurned at every kindness or emolument, submitted to his acceptance and consideration : they even offered him one thousand pounds, English, and two benefits whenever he chose to take them ; but all would not do, though they certainly would have been losers by his acceptance, but their situation was desperate ; therefore all they could do was right if by any means they could have effectually prevented such an opposition. Mossop's pride and obstinacy was however bent on monarchy, and so he was the cause of mutual ruin, but he at last suffered a peculiar degree of punishment.

He had saved a decent fortune, and by the absence of Barry, could have commanded a first station in London, at either theatre, whenever he pleased, or wished a change from Dublin ; but his pride was predominant over reason, so he prostrated fame, fortune, health and peace of mind, headlong at the shrine of vanity, where sycophants hailed him with songs of triumph in full chorus, but his festal days were few and not to be envied.

Barry and Woodward on this act of hostility being put into actual force, were from necessity glad to secure Mrs. Abington ; and I do suppose, however she might fear foul play from Mr. Barry and Mrs. Dancer, thought Woodward to act with was a great point, much better than being at Mossop's new theatre without such a partner to support her; Mossop being out of her walk, and Woodward the comedian. She therefore depended on his interest and candour for her consequence in the comic line.

CHAPTER III.

Admiration excited in Ireland by Mrs. Abington—Mrs. Abington and
the M.P. for Newry; Death of the latter, Provision made for Mrs. A.—
Return to Drury Lane—Murphy's Inscription of the Way to Keep Him
to Mrs. Abington—His flattering recognition of her services—The
Provoked Wife—Plain Dealer—Clandestine Marriage—Rule a Wife—
Beggar's Opera—Romeo and Juliet—Virgin Unmasked—Cymon—English
Merchant—Provoked Husband—Country Girl—School for Lovers—
Widow'd Wife—All in the Wrong—False Delicacy—Richard III.—
Like Master like Man—Funeral—Lottery—Merchant of Venice—
Hypocrite—No Wit like a Woman's—Shakespeare's Jubilee—Foote and
Garrick—Mrs. Abington as Comedy—The Stratagem—School for Rakes
—Jealous Wife—Confederacy—Merry Wives—Double Gallant—Careless
Husband—West Indian—Way of the World—High Life Below Stairs—
Twin Rivals—Mrs. Abington in Paris—Horace Walpole—Twelfth Night
—Hamlet—The Lady's Last Stake—Linca's Travels—Revival of The
Chances, Mrs. Abington as Second Constantia—George II. and the
Theatre—The Committee—Fair Quaker of Deal—Gamesters—Epilogue
to the Gamesters—Various plays, as the Frenchified Lady, Merope,
Albumazar, Prologue to last—Rule a Wife—School for Wives.

Mrs. Abington's success in Ireland was universally allowed to
have been most unqualified, writers and critics of all kinds vied
with each other in expressing their admiration of her talents and
rendering to her a suitable tribute of applause.   From the first
to the last of her five years' visit, her career had been triumphant,
her peculiar ability for the parts in which she appeared asserting
itself beyond contradiction or controversy, and winning from the
play-going public the highest approbation.   " To the courteous
and hospitable inhabitants of the sister-isle, she needed no other
credentials than the super-natural talent with which she was
gifted by nature, and that being called forth by the genial hand,
continued fostering of public applause on the Dublin stage (the
best seminary for those of London), she not only shooted forward,
but even out-bloomed the fairest conceived hopes of her excelling
in Thalia's department.   In this admired point of view it is not
to be wondered, that, among a people, one of whose characteristics
is gallantry, many of the young fashionable gentry and nobility
paid their complimentary addresses to so attractive an object,
and to which it is hard for female vanity not to listen."
Whether she might have hearkened with too encouraging an
indulgence to such addresses, or, that her husband (who had

accompanied her to Ireland) was, by insinuation from others, or suggestion from himself, induced to believe she did, is what we cannot take upon us to say, but it is certain that when she became universally popular, he became extremely jealous and conceived an antipathy against her. Her indignation was aroused, and she affected to return this treatment with marks of contempt and indignation, till, by degrees, what was at first but a semblance in her, became at last to be a fixed reality, which by his subsequent conduct her patron rendered immovable, whereupon ensued the separation and agreement already mentioned.

Availing herself of the liberty afforded by this separation, Mrs. Abington appears to have regarded herself as a single woman again, and apparently was looked upon in the same light by others. In order to rid herself of the crowd of admirers who daily surrounded her, and emboldened by her husband's absence, did not scruple openly to declare their love, and to enjoy quiet under what she called an honourable protection (since the circumstances of her position prevented her accepting any proposals of marriage), she yielded at last to the solicitations of a gentleman of family, fortune and learning, who had made the tour of Europe, and was Member of Parliament for Newry in the county of Down.

This connection, brought about through an approving choice of the mind on both sides, rather than the gratification of any other wish, the pleasure arising from this intercourse, became gradually so intense, that he delighted in no company so much as hers, each was a great and irresistible attraction to the other and while she found herself unable to withdraw herself from his company, he was charmed in cultivating a mind happily disposed to receive and profit by his instruction, enjoying a singular satisfaction in reading, explaining, and communicating to her every kind of knowledge.

Business calling this gentleman to England shortly after, an opportunity was afforded Mrs. Abington of re-visiting her native country. The great reputation she had at once achieved in Ireland, had very speedily attracted the attention of English managers, and Mr. Garrick had thought it worth his while to make her what was then considered an extravagant offer to return to Drury-lane, an offer she declined accepting until Garrick returned from Italy and re-occupied his own house. Meanwhile her protector's state of health became so bad as to give rise to serious apprehensions respecting the future, and impelled by a sense of duty and affection, she attended him to Bath and some other places that, it was hoped, might assist in his recovery, but a constitutional malady, under which he had laboured from his infancy, at last getting the better of him and threatening him with the approach of that final tribute, which is to be paid at one time or other, by all mortal beings, he bethought himself seriously of leaving out of the reach of adversity, a faithful friend and companion who had devoted herself to him, and whose behaviour, during his last illness, was such as the most heroic matron might not be ashamed to copy. His heirs afterwards discharged, in a very honourable manner, the provision he had made for her, and she was also favoured by the family with a notice that is rarely the consequence of an attachment of such a nature.

Accepting Mr. Garrick's pressing invitations and offer of what was then considered the liberal salary of £5 per week, Mrs. Abington agreed to return to Drury-lane, and resolved when her grief on account of her loss in the death of her lover was somewhat assuaged, to exert her utmost efforts to reach the highest pinnacle of fame in the particular line of business to which she had shewn herself so peculiarly adapted. The difficulty of finding a good part for her, however, seemed at first to present a formidable obstacle to her occupation of the position for which she was adapted. Nearly all those in which she had been so successful in Dublin, were in the possession of Mrs. Clive and Mrs. Pritchard, the Widow Belmour in Murphy's comedy "The Way to Keep Him," was the only one of any consequence, open to her. "With all her blushing honours thick about her," she made her first appearance for five years in this character, November 27th, 1765, and not only confirmed the report of her former reputation, but drew that applause from the author (as expressed in the edition of 1787) which will be a lasting test of her intrinsic merit.

MR. MURPHY TO MRS. ABINGTON.

Madam—You will be surprised at this distance of time, and in this public manner, to receive an answer to a very polite letter, which you addressed to me in the course of the last summer at Yarmouth. In a strain of vivacity, which always belongs to you, you invite me to write again for the stage. You will tell me that having gone through the comedies of the "Way to Keep Him," "All in the Wrong," and "Three Weeks after Marriage," you now want more from the same hand. I am not bound, you say, by my resolution, signified in a Prologue about ten years ago, to take my leave of the dramatic muse. At the perjuries of Poets, as well as lovers, Jove laughs; and the public you think, will be ready to give me a general release from the promise. All this is very flattering. If the following scenes, at the end of five and twenty years, still continue to be a part of the public amusement, I know to what cause I am to ascribe it. Those graces of action, with which you adorn whatever you undertake, have given to the piece a degree of brilliancy, and even novelty, as often as you have repeated it. I am not unmindful of the performers who first obtained for the author the favour of the town; a Garrick, a Yates, a Cibber, united their abilities; and who can forget Mrs. Clive? They have all passed away, and the comedy might have passed with them, if you had not so frequently placed it in a conspicuous light.

The truth is, without such talents as yours, all that the poet writes is a dead letter—he designs for representation, but it is the performer that gives to the draught, however justly traced, a form, a spirit, a countenance, and a mind. All this you have done for the Widow Belmour; and that excellence in your art, which you are known to possess, can, no doubt, lend the same animation to any new character. But, alas! I have none to offer. That tinder in the poet's mind, which, as Doctor Young says, takes fire from every spark, I have not found, even though you have endeavoured to kindle the flame. Could I write as you can act, I should be proud to obey your commands; but after a long disuse, how shall I recover the train of thinking necessary for plot, humour, incident, and character?

In the place of novelty, permit me to request that The Way to Keep Him may be inscribed to you. You are entitled to it, Madam, for your talents have made the play your own. A Dedication, I grant, at this period of time, comes rather late; but being called upon for a new edition, I have retouched the dialogue, and perhaps so reformed the whole, that in its present state it may be deemed less unworthy of your acceptance. It is, therefore, my wish, that this address may in future attend the comedy, to remain (as long as such a thing can remain), a tribute due to the genius of Mrs. Abington, and a mark of that esteem with which I subscribe myself,

   Madam,
    Your real admirer,
      And most obedient servant,
Lincoln's Inn,   ARTHUR MURPHY.
  25th Nov., 1785.

"Here we cannot but pause to think of the inward satisfaction Mrs. Abington must necessarily feel on her return to Drury-lane theatre; when she had to reflect that by her own spirited, yet prudent conduct, she had been the architect of her own fame and growing fortune. Had she, like other young actresses, been content to vegetate in the soil where she was first planted (and which, perhaps, it would have been prudent for another person to have so advised her), time and chance might have raised her to an eligible situation; but true genius, generally speaking, is its best adviser. She knew best what she could do, and what another might call presumption, she found from her feelings to be the call of nature; she had spirit as well as judgment to obey that call, and her grateful mistress, ever true to her votaries, did not neglect to cultivate the sentiments she inspired.

Dec. 5th, of this same year, was performed by command,"The Provoked Wife."

Sir John Brute...	GARRICK.
Lady Brute	MRS. CIBBER.
Lady Fanciful	MRS. ABINGTON.

The *Public Advertiser* for Dec. 2nd says : "Mrs. Cibber is come to town and so well recovered as to be able to appear in Belvidera, the latter end of the week." This, however, proved the last time but one that her name was in the bill.

Dec. 7th was revived after twenty years, "The Plain Dealer," considerably modified by Bickerstaffe. "Notwithstanding the excellence of "The Plain Dealer," it could not well have been performed before a modern audience without alterations. Bickerstaffe is entitled to some degree of credit for reforming the exceptional parts without materially mutilating the plot— he ought, however, to have retained much more of the original dialogue—instead of which he has foisted in several short insipid make-shift scenes of his own."—(Genest.) With the above was performed "The Virgin Unmasked," (first time in five years) Mrs. Abington playing the part of Miss Lucy.

Dec. 13th, "The Provoked Wife" performed, Mrs. Abington as previously in the part of Lady Fanciful, with Mrs. Cibber as Lady Brute—her name in the bill for the last time.

Feb. 20th, 1766, "The Clandestine Marriage" performed, Mrs. Abington acted Betty in the play and Miss Crotchet in the epilogue, but when the play was printed, she would not suffer her name to be put to such small parts. Genest says "this was ridiculous, as her name had been in the bills—I have the real bill for the seventh night of "The Clandestine Marriage," with Mrs. Abington's name in it."

April 8th, "Rule a Wife" performed, Mrs. Abington playing Estifania at her own benefit.

April 14th, at Miss Wright's benefit, "The Beggar's Opera," Lucy by Mrs. Abington.

May 2nd, Romeo and Juliet, with Catherine and Petruchio, by Mrs. Abington and King; Grumio, Yates.

May 10th, "The Way of the World," Millamant, Mrs. Abington.

Sept. 25th, "The Beggar's Opera," Lucy, Mrs. Abington.

Oct. 10th, "The Provoked Wife."

Sir John Brute...	GARRICK.
Constant	BENSLEY.
Heartfree	PALMER.
Razor	YATES.
Lady Fanciful	MRS. ABINGTON.
Lady Brute	MRS. PALMER.
Belinda	MISS PLYM.
Mademoiselle	MRS. CROSS.

Nov. 7th, "The Virgin Unmasked," Mrs. Abington as Miss Lucy.

Jan. 2nd, 1767, Cymon, never acted.

Cymon	VERNON.
Linco	KING.
Merlin	BENSLEY.
Dorus	PARSONS.
Damon and Dorilas	FAWCETT AND FOX.
Demon of Revenge	CHAMPNESS.
Sylvia .:.	MRS. ARNE.
Urganda	MRS. BADDELEY
Fatima	MRS. ABINGTON.
Dorcas	MRS. BRADSHAW.
1st Shepherdess	MISS REYNOLDS.
2nd do.	MISS PLYM.

"Cymon was acted with great success—a third edition of it was printed in 1767—King, Parsons, and Mrs. Abington played particularly well. This dramatic romance, in five acts, is founded on Dryden's tale of Cymon and Iphigenia. It is so generally attributed to Garrick, that there can be no doubt of his being the author. As a first piece it is contemptible : if it had been brought out in two acts as a mere vehicle for songs, scenery, &c., it might have past without censure." (Genest.)

Feb. 21st, "The English Merchant," never acted. Genest says, "This is a very good comedy, by Colman ; he dedicated it to Voltaire, on whose Scotchwoman he had founded his piece. Voltaire at first published his play under a fictitious name, and pretended that he had translated it from a comedy written by the author of Douglas. Colman has not made any very material alterations in the plot, but he has improved the play in many points." Davies says that two celebrated performers (King, who played Spatter, and Mrs. Abington, who played Lady Alton), expected to have been hissed on the first night, but were well received.

April 22nd, Mrs. Abington's benefit, was performed " The Way to Keep Him," with " Marriage-a-la-Mode, or Conjugal Douceurs." This is supposed to have been some piece in which Mrs. Abington had acted in Ireland.

Sept. 18, " The Provoked Husband."

Lord Townly ... REDDISH—his first appearance at
Lady Townly ... MRS. ABINGTON.   [Drury-lane.

Oct. 28, " The Virgin Unmasked," Miss Lucy, Mrs. Abington.

Nov. 16th, " The Country Girl," Mrs. Abington.

Critics are of opinion she ought to have had the character before as she had been highly successful with similar parts in Ireland.

Nov. 23rd, " The School for Lovers,"Araminta, Mrs. Abington.

Dec. 5th, " The Widow'd Wife," never acted.

Frederick Mellmott	... ...	REDDISH.
Syllogism	... ...	KING.
General Mellmott	... ...	HOLLAND.
Colonel Camply	... ...	AIKEN.
Alderman Lombard	... ...	LOVE.
Furnival	... ...	J. PALMER.
Lord Courtly	... ...	J. AIKIN.
Dr. Mineral	... ...	DODD.
Mrs. Mildmay	... ...	MRS. PRITCHARD.
Narcissa	... ...	MRS. ABINGTON.
Sophia	... ...	MRS. PALMER.
Sift	... ...	MRS. CLIVE.
Susan	... ...	MRS. BRADSHAW.

" The piece was acted 14 or 15 times—it is a moderate comedy by Kenrick—the dialogue is better than the plot "

Jan. 19th, 1768, was performed " All in the Wrong."

Belinda ... ... MRS. ABINGTON.

Jan. 23rd, Never acted, " False Delicacy," a sentimental comedy by Kelly, good in its way but narrowly escaping the charge

of excessive dullness.   Mrs. Abington played Lady Betty
Lambton.   The object of the play was to ridicule "False
Delicacy."

April 6th, Mrs. Abington's benefit, "The Way to Keep Him,"
Mrs. Abington as the Widow Belmour.   Also the new comedy
of "National Prejudice," with Mrs Abington, Miss Reynolds,
Reddish, Cautherley, and J. Palmer.

April 12th, Reddish's benefit, "Richard III.," with "Like
Master, like Man," altered from "Vanburgh's Mistake," (never
acted there).   Genest says: "Mrs. Baddeley and Mrs. Abington
probably acted Leonora and Jackinta.   This farce came out in
Ireland—perhaps before Reddish left that kingdom—it was
printed at Dublin in 1770.   "The Mistake" is so good a play
that it ought not to have been cut down to a farce—besides the
thing is done in an absurd manner—in the 2nd act, Leonora
threatens that she would repulse Carlos for the future, but she
certainly had not repulsed him when she makes her exit—yet
Carlos enters immediately and says—"repulsed again! this is
not to be borne."

April 14th, Cautherley's benefit, "The Funeral."

Lady Harriet	MRS. ABINGTON.

Oct. 31st, "The Lottery."

Lady Lace...	MRS. ABINGTON.

Nov. 5th, "The Merchant of Venice."

Portia	MRS. ABINGTON (1st time.)

Nov. 17th, "The Hypocrite." (never acted.)

Dr. Cantwell	KING.
Darnley	REDDISH.
Col. Lambert	JEFFERSON.
Leyward	CAUTHERLEY.
Maw-worm	WELTON.
Sir John Lambert	PACKER.
Charlotte	MRS. ABINGTON.
Lady Lambert...	MRS. W. BARRY.
Old Lady Lambert...	MRS. BRADSHAW.

"This is a very good alteration of the Nonjuror.   Charlotte is
the best drawn coquette and the most defensible one on the
stage, though the part had been well performed by Mrs. Oldfield
originally, and since her time with great applause and approbation by Mrs. Woffington and Mrs. Pritchard, yet it is impossible

to conceive that more gaiety, ease, humour, eloquence and grace, could have been assumed by any actress than by Mrs. Abington in this part—(Davies) she had acted Maria in Ireland."

Nov. 21st, " The Provoked Husband."

Lady Townly ... ... MRS. ABINGTON.

Dec. 14th, " The Provoked Wife."

Lady Fanciful ... ... MRS. ABINGTON.

Jan. 7th, 1769, " The Merchant of Venice."

Portia ... ... MRS. ABINGTON.

March 28, Mrs. Abington's benefit, "The Hypocrite, fourteenth time, with " No Wit like a Woman's." (Never acted.)

March 31st, " No Wit like a Woman's."

" Taken from George Dangin of Moliere; Modely, Palmer; Vintage, Weston; Symon, Moody; Mrs. Vintage, Mrs. Abington. Not printed."

In September, 1769, a Jubilee in honour of Shakespeare was celebrated at Stratford, under the direction of Garrick.

Foote, either from envy of Garrick's taking the lead in this business, or from thinking that he conducted it with too much vanity and self-ostentation, looked with a jealous eye upon the whole, and hence took every little occasion, in squibs, sarcasms, and bon-mots, to arraign the projector's taste and management.

This conduct, however, passed off with a laugh on both sides, till the winter following; when, finding that Garrick meant to convert his Jubilee into an object of profit, by bringing out a representation of it on the stage, Foote's spleen could be restrained no longer—he played off all his powers of ridicule on every part of the subject, both in company and in the public papers—particularly on the ode on erecting a statue to Shakespeare, in which he pointed out some errors and inaccuracies with such force of humour, as gained the greatest part of the laughter on his side.

He carried his satire still further; for, finding that the entertainment of " The Stratford Jubilee " ran to ninety nights, in that season, his jealousy became so strong, that he intended to bring out a mock procession in imitation of it, and introduce Garrick himself on the stage as the principal figure. In this procession, a man was to be dressed out so as to resemble Garrick as much as possible, in the character of Steward of the

Jubilee, with his wand, white topped gloves, and the mulberry-tree medallion of Shakespeare hanging at his breast; while some ragamuffin in the procession should address him in two well-known lines of the grossest flattery. To this, Garrick's representative was to make no other answer, but clap his arms, like the wings of a cock, and crow out, Cock-a-doodle-doo!

Garrick had early intelligence of his whole scheme, and the uneasiness which he felt upon the occasion could not be dissembled—he dreaded public ridicule as the most painful of all misfortunes; and in the hands of such a man as Foote, he apprehended the decay, perhaps the ruin, of that reputation which was ever dear to him, and which he had been raising for so many years. However, suddenly this mighty project fell to the ground; a nobleman, the mutual friend of both, seeing Garrick so very unhappy about this menaced caricature, prevailed upon Foote to abandon the design—the parties met as if by accident, at the house of this nobleman, when alighting at the same time from their chariots at his lordship's door, and exchanging significant looks at each other, Garrick broke silence first, by asking, " Is it war or peace? "—Oh! peace by all means said the other, with much apparent good will, and the day was spent in great cordiality." (Cook and Davies.)

The *New Monthly Magazine* for Feb. 1838, says : Mrs. Abington represented comedy in the pageant of the Jubilee, in 1769.

" Delightful, ever charming fair,
Whose presence ev'n the sons of care
    With brows unfolded own,
How can the raptures be express'd
Of merry souls to see thee placed
    Upon the comic throne ?
There long despotic may'st thou reign,
And not a patriot will complain
    Thy tyranny is grievous !
No, Britons, let us all unite,
And join in comedy's delight,
    Ere Abington must leave us."

Oct. 6th, " The Stratagem."
    Mrs. Sullen   ...   .   Mrs. Abington.

Oct. 10th, " The Provoked Wife."
    Lady Fanciful ...   .   Mrs. Abington.

Oct. 14, The " School for Rakes," with the Jubilee.   In the

piece will be introduced the pageant as it was intended for
Stratford-upou-Avon. Characters in pageant.

Benedick	...	...	...	...	GARRICK.
Beatrice	...	...	...	...	MISS POPE.
Touchstone	...	...	...	...	KING.
Richard III.	...	...	...	...	HOLLAND.
Romeo	...	...	...	...	BRERETON.
Hamlet	...	...	...	...	CAUTHERLEY.
Falstaff	...	...	...	...	LOVE.
Lear	...	...	...	...	REDDISH.
Antony	...	...	...	...	AIKIN.
Portia	...	...	...	...	MRS. W. BARRY.
Apollo	...	...	...	...	VERNON.
Tragic Muse	...	...	...	...	MRS. BARRY.
Comic Muse	...	...	...	...	MRS. ABINGTON.

Davies says that Stevens, to the great annoyance of Garrick,
turned the whole business of the real Jubilee at Stratford into
ridicule, and indeed it seems to have been a foolish affair, better
calculated to gratify Garrick's vanity, than to do honour to
Shakespeare. The Drury-lane Jubilee was very pleasing in the
representation and was acted through the whole season to
crowded houses.

Oct. 26th, "Merchant of Venice."
  Portia... ... ... MRS. ABINGTON.

Dec. 4th, "The Jealous Wife."
  Mr. & Mrs. Oakly... REDDISH & MRS. ABINGTON.

Dec. 8th, "Confederacy."
  Corinna ... ... MRS. ABINGTON.

Dec. 16th, "Merry Wives."
  Ford ... . AIKIN (1st time.)
  Slender ... ... CAUTHERLEY (1st time.)
  Mrs. Ford ... ... MRS. ABINGTON (1st time.)

Dec. 23rd, "Love for Love."—(not acted for five years.)
  Miss Prue... ... ... MRS. ABINGTON.

Jan. 16th, 1770, "The Double Gallant."—(not acted six years.)
  Lady Sadlife ... ... MRS. ABINGTON.

Jan. 25th, "The Careless Husband."
  Lady Betty Modish... ... ... MRS. ABINGTON.

March 1st, "Rule a Wife,"
  Leon ... ... GARRICK.
  Estifania ... ... MRS. ABINGTON.

March 24th, "Cymon," with (not acted eight years) "Frenchified Lady," never in Paris.

Melantha ... ...   MRS. ABINGTON.

Feb. 19th, 1771, "The West Indian." (never acted.)

Belcour	KING.
Major O'Flaherty	MOODY.
Stockwell	AIKIN.
Varland	PARSONS.
Captain Dudley	PACKER.
Ensign Dudley...	CAUTHERLEY.
Fulmer	BADDELEY.
Charlotte Rusport	MRS. ABINGTON.
Lady Rusport	MRS. HOPKINS.
Louisa Dudley	MRS. BADDELEY.
Mrs. Fulmer	MRS. EGERTON.

"This has always been considered as Cumberland's best play—it is not a little remarkable, that in his own life he calls it a fortunate comedy, and almost gives the preference to "The Fashionable Lover,"—it must indeed be allowed, that, though the piece is deservedly a favourite both on and off the stage, yet it cannot be said to be a copy from life—the foibles, the humours, and real manners of a West Indian planter are not delineated with truth and accuracy."—(Murphy.)

"Barry was extremely desirous to play the Irish Major, and Garrick was very doubtful how to decide, for Moody was then an actor but little known and at a low salary—after a long deliberation he gave his decree for Moody with considerable repugnance, qualifying his preference of the latter with reasons that in no respect reflected on the merits of Barry, but he did not see him in the whole character of O'Flaherty; there were certain points of humour where he thought it likely he might fail, and in that case his failure, like his name, would be more conspicuous than Moody's; in short, Moody would take pains; it might make him, it might mar the other; so Moody had it and succeeded to the utmost wish of the manager and author. Mrs. Abington, with a few salvos on the score of condescension, took Charlotte Rusport, and though she would not allow it to be anything but a sketch, yet she made it a character by her inimitable acting."—(Cumberland.)

"Cumberland seems to forget himself strangely in what he says about Moody—he had acted all the Irish characters for several years, and had particularly distinguished himself in "The Jubilee." Garrick's doubt perhaps arose from his fear that

Moody would not be sufficiently the gentleman, and that Barry would not be sufficiently comic."—(Genest.)

March 14th, "Cymon," with (not acted fourteen years) "The Author."

Mrs. Cadwallader ... ... MRS. ABINGTON.

March 18th, "The Way of the World," and "High Life Below Stairs," Mrs. Abington's benefit.

Millamant in the former, Kitty in the latter... ...
MRS. ABINGTON.

March 21st, Miss Pope's benefit, "The Funeral."

Lady Harriet ... ... MRS. ABINGTON.

April 5th, Moody's benefit, "The Twin Rivals."

Aurelia ... ... MRS. ABINGTON.

May 7th, I. Sparks's benefit, "The Provoked Husband."

Lady Townly ... ... MRS. ABINGTON.

In 1771, Mrs. Abington paid a visit to Paris, and we accordingly hear no more of her performances till her return to Drury-lane in the autumn. Just now we come upon some correspondence with Horace Walpole, which was continued in after years. An undated letter, probably written before she started for Paris, says: "Mr. Walpole cannot express how much he is mortified that he cannot accept of Mrs. Abington's obliging invitation, as he had engaged company to dine with him on Sunday, at Strawberry Hill, whom he would put off, if not foreigners, who are leaving England. Mr. Walpole hopes, however, that this accident will not prevent an acquaintance which his admiration of Mrs. Abington's genius has made him long desire, and which he hopes to cultivate at Strawberry Hill, when her leisure will give him leave to trouble her with an invitation."

While in Paris she received the following:—

To MRS. ABINGTON,
PARIS, SEPTEMBER 1ST, 1771.

If I had known Madam of your being at Paris, before I heard it from Colonel Blaquiere, I should certainly have prevented your flattering invitation, and have offered you any services that could depend on my acquaintance here. It is plain I am old and live with very old folks, when I did not hear of your arrival. However, Madam, I have not that fault at least of a veteran, the thinking nothing equal to what they admired in their youth. I do impartial justice to your merit, and fairly allow it not only equal to that of any actress I have seen, but believe the present age will not be in the wrong, if they hereafter prefer it to those they may live to see.

Your allowing me to wait on you in London, Madam, will make me some amends for the loss I have had here, and I shall take an early opportunity of assuring you how much.

I am, Madam,

Your most obliged humble servant,

HOR. WALPOLE.

We have now reached the autumn of 1771, and find Mrs. Abington again at Drury Lane playing her well-known part of the Widow Belmour in "The Way to Keep Him," on the 31st of October.

Dec. 13th, "Twelfth Night" performed, Mrs. Abington as Olivia. Reported as very well acted.

Dec. 30th, "The Country Girl," by Mrs. Abington.

Jan. 8th, 1772, "Hamlet."

| Hamlet | ... | ... | ... | ... | ... | GARRICK. |
| Ophelia | ... | ... | ... | ... | ... | MRS. ABINGTON. |

Feb. 5th, "Hamlet."

| Hamlet | ... | ... | ... | ... | ... | GARRICK. |
| Ophelia | ... | ... | ... | ... | ... | MRS. ABINGTON. |

Feb. 29th, "The Lottery."

Lord Lace	...	...	...	...	KING.
Stocks	...	...	...	...	PARSONS.
Lovermore	...	...	...	...	BANNISTER.
Lady Lace	...	...	...	...	MRS. ABINGTON.

March 30th, "Lady's Last Stake," Mrs. Abington's benefit.

Lord Wronglove	...	REDDISH.
Lord George Brilliant	KING (first time).
Sir Friendly Moral	...	AIKIN.
Lady Wronglove	...	MRS. HOPKINS.
Miss Notable	...	...	MRS. ABINGTON (1st time there).
Mrs. Conquest	...	MISS YOUNGE (first time).
Lady Gentle	...	...	MRS. EGERTON.

With Linca's Travels. Pit and boxes laid together.

April 4th, "Double Gallant," Miss Pope's benefit.

Atall	...	...	...	...	...	KING.
Lady Sadlife	...	...	...	...	MRS. ABINGTON.
Lady Dainty	...	...	...	...	MISS POPE.

April 9th, " As you like it " and " Author."

Mrs. Cadwallader ... ... MRS. ABINGTON.

On the return of Mrs. Abington to England, some favourable circumstances concurred to bring her forward in characters that gave additional lustre to her reputation. One of the earliest of these was that of the Second Constantia in the revived comedy of "The Chances." As the history of the revival of this play contains not only the circumstances that led to Mrs. Abington's introduction to this character, but also some curious anecdotes of royalty, we shall give it entire from Mr. Davies's " Life of Garrick," a work replete with great theatrical knowledge and judicious criticism.

"Amongst his many kingly virtues, George II. could not enumerate the patronage of science and love of vertu. Poetry, painting, sculpture, and all the imitative arts were neither understood nor encouraged by him. When Hogarth presented him with his admirable picture of the "March to Hounslow," he thought the painter well rewarded with the donation of a guinea. Garrick's excellence in acting was as little admired by his Majesty as the humour of Hogarth."

It was with difficulty the good king could be persuaded that he who represented so strongly the atrocious acts of Richard III. could in reality be an honest man. However, Taswell, who acted the Lord Mayor of London in the same play, attracted his attention : the king thought him an excellent city magistrate, and laughed heartily at his burlesque oratory. The players indeed by their dressing of the Mayor and his brethren, and giving the parts to a comic actor and a parcel of scene men, seem to have designedly thrown a kind of ridicule, where the author certainly never intended any. However, the king had no aversion to the entertainments of the stage, and he generally bespoke a play twice or thrice in a twelvemonth. But it appeared that he was best pleased with these dramatic pieces which abounded in low humour and extravagant plot. The London Cuckholds and Fair Quaker of Deal were in more estimation with him than the best written comedies in the English language.

The reader will not, I hope, be displeased if I should record an anecdote of the royal taste for scenes of a peculiar cast. He had, when Prince of Wales, seen the tragedy of " Venice Preserved," but on his reading the play, he found the character of Aquilina, the Venetian courtezan, had been entirely omitted, and very little of Antonio, the foolish orator, her lover, preserved. His Highness was so diverted with the ridiculous dotages of the

D

old speechmaker, and the perverse and petulant humours of his mistress, that he sent for one of the managers, and ordered him to restore the long-exploded scenes of Antonio and Aquilina. Mrs. Horton, who was then a beautiful young actress, played the part of the courtezan, and the facetious Mr. William Pinkethman acted Antonio; but whether the revived scenes gave pleasure to anybody but the Royal Person who commanded them, I could not learn.

The play of "The Chances," as altered from Beaumont and Fletcher, by Villiers, Duke of Buckingham, had been thrown out of the common list of plays for above twenty-five years. The King happened to recollect that Wilkes and Oldfield had greatly diverted him in that comedy, and he asked one of his courtiers why it was never played. Mr. Garrick, as soon as he learned the King's pleasure to see "The Chances," immediately set about reforming the play so as to render it exceptionable in language and action.

The manager's great difficulty was how to cast the part of the Second Constantia, in such a manner, as that she might bear some resemblance to the first. Mrs. Pritchard was the only actress in the company who had in a superior degree, much vivacity, variety of humour, and engaging action; but this lady was become so bulky in her person, that she could not be mistaken for Miss Macklin, whose figure was elegant, and who acted the first Constantia. But could Mr. Garrick have surmounted this difficulty, Mrs. Cibber, by a clause in her articles, claimed a right to choose any character she pleased to act in a new or revived play. This actress, whose tones of voice were so expressive of all the tender passions, and who was by nature formed for tragic representation, was uncommonly desirous of acting characters of gaiety and humour, to which she was an absolute stranger. She had no idea of Comedy, but such as implied a representation of childish simplicity.

Mr. Garrick knew that it was impossible to divert her from the resolution to play Constantia, and therefore determined to give way to her humour, till the want of applause should admonish her to resign the part.

I need not recall to the reader's mind the great delight which Mr. Garrick gave the public in Don John. Mrs. Cibber soon grew tired of a part to which the audience afforded no signs of approbation; Miss Haughton, a young actress, succeeded her for a short time, and merited a good share of applause. But it was in the sequel, in Mrs. Abington, that Mr. Garrick met with a Constantia who disputed the palm of victory with him. She so happily assumed all the gay airs, peculiar oddities, and various attitudes of an agreeable and frolicsome mad-cap, that the audience were kept in constant good humour and merriment, which they recompensed by the loudest applause, through all the several scenes in which she acted. The king commanded The Chances, and seemed to enjoy the performance."

April 27th, " The Committee."

Ruth ... ... MRS. ABINGTON.

May 12th, " The Fair Quaker of Deal."

Arabella ... ... MRS. ABINGTON.

June 10th, Reddish and Mrs. Abington as Mr. and Mrs. Oakley.

Oct. 30th, " The Gamesters," not acted for 14 years.

Wilding ... ... KING.
Hazard ... ... REDDISH.
Barnacle ... ... PARSONS.
Nephew ... ... DODD.
Penelope ... ... MRS. ABINGTON.
Mrs. Wilding ... ... MISS YOUNGE.

Epilogue to the revived comedy of " The Gamesters."
Spoken by MRS. ABINGTON.

" Critics, before you rise, one word, I pray ;
You cannot to a female sure say nay !—
I'll make a short excuse for what I've done,
And then to church with Master Hazard run :
Yes, run I say, nay fly, my zeal to prove,
Fly to the Indies—with the man I love !
Love, a choice plant, once native of this soil,
Grew, spread, and blossom'd without care or toil ;
'Twas through the land in such perfection kept,
That ivy-like, around the heart it crept ;
Each honest-feeling bosom nurs'd the flow'r
So sweet, it often proved the happiest dow'r ;
Till folks of taste, their genius to display,
Brought in exotics ; while to sad decay
Poor love is fallen, cast like a weed away !
I will revive the plant in spite of fashions ;
The heart is dead without that best of passions ;
Aye, but says Surly (there I see him sit
Glancing a frown upon me from the pit),
I am for loving, Miss, as well as you ;
But not a dice-box—that will never do !
Who draws for husbands, these, with open eyes
Puts in a lottery without one prize !
Sir—by your leave—your praise I wish to merit,

For stepping forth with more than female spirit !
Am not I brave, amid the tempest's war,
To plunge and bring a drowning man to shore ?
But should the monstre so ungrateful prove,
When I have saved and warm'd him with my love,
To let his former sins his heart entice
And leave my rattling for the rattling dice !
I'll strike a bargain, and I say done first,
As soon as e'er my wretched spouse is hears'd ;
For if he wear his worthless life away,
Watching all night, and fretting all the day ;
E'en let him go, his loss your gain secures,
The widow and ten thousand shall be yours !
Our youths are so fin'd down with fashions new,
I'd rather chuse a surly man like you."

Feb. 18th, 1773, " The Double Gallant."

Lady Sadlife   ...   .   Mrs. ABINGTON.

March 23rd, For King's Benefit, " Double Dealer."

Lady Froth   ...   .   Mrs. ABINGTON.

March 27th, " The Gamesters " and " Frenchified Lady,"
Mrs. Abington's benefit.

Melantha ...   .   Mrs. ABINGTON.

April 3rd, " Merope " and " The Intriguing Chambermaid,"
Miss Younge's benefit.

Lettice   ...   .   Mrs. ABINGTON.

April 13th, " Fashionable Lover " and " Intriguing Chambermaid, by Mrs. Abington.   Love's benefit.

April 21st, " Chances," revived.

Second Constantia ...   .   Mrs. ABINGTON.

Oct. 19th, " Albumazer," not acted 26 years.

Sulpitia   ...   .   Mrs. ABINGTON.

"Albumazer" was revived in 1668, it was now revived with
alterations by Garrick—they are not material, but one of them
must not be passed over without notice—in the original, Ronca,
looking into the perspicil, says, I see the Jesuits at Rome, and
what they write and do.—This Garrick has changed to—"I see
the Jesuits like a swarm of bees all buzzing, just turned out."—
Pandolfo. " A good riddance "—this allusion to the suppression
of the Jesuits in 1773, is introduced in this old comedy with
peculiar impropriety."

Prologue to the revived comedy of " Albumazer."

Spoken by MRS. ABINGTON.

" In times of old, by this old play we see,
Our Ancestors, poor souls, though brave and free,
Believed in spirits and astrology!
'Twas by the *stars* they prosper'd, or miscarried;
Thro' *them* grew rich, or poor; were hang'd or married;
And if their wives were naught, then they were born
Under the *Ram*, or *Bull*, or *Capricorn*!
When our great grandmamas had made a slip,
(Their shoes with higher heels would often trip)
The rose and lily left their cheeks——'twas duty
To curse their *Planets* and destroy their beauty.
Such ign'rance, with faith in *Stars*, prevails;
Our faces never change, they tell no tales;
Or should a husband, rather unpolite
Lock up our persons, and our roses blight;
When once set free again, there's nothing in it,
We can be *ros'd* and *lily'd* in a minute;
Fly all abroad, be taken into favour,
And be as fresh and frolicsome as ever!
To heav'nly bodies we have no relation,
The *Star* that rules us is our *inclination*!
Govern'd by that, our *earthly* bodies move,
Quite unconnected with the things above.
Two young ones love—a chaise to Scotland carries 'em.
The *Star* lend light, but *inclination* marries 'em.
When passion cools, and flame is turned to smother,
They curse no *Stars*—but Scotland and each other!
To walk i'th dark no Belles now make a fuss,
No Spectres or Hobgoblins frighten us!
No, says Old Crab, of Fops the last Editions,
Pray, Madam, what are they but Apparitions?
So slim, so pale, so dress'd from foot to head,
Half girl, half boy, half living, and half dead,
They are not flesh and blood, but walking gingerbread.
Mere flimsy beings kept alive by art,
"They come like shadows, and they'll so depart."
O fye, for shame! said I—He turned about,
And turned us topsy turvey, inside out:
Rail'd at our Sex, then curs'd the *Stars*, and swore—
But you're alarmed I see, I'll say no more:
Old doating fools from *Stars* derive all evil,
Nor search their hearts to find the little devil:
Ladies take counsel, crush the mischief there;
Lay but the *Spirit*, you'll be wise—as fair."

Oct. 22nd, " Rule a Wife."
Estifania ...   .   MRS. ABINGTON.

Dec. 11th, " The School for Wives," never acted.
Miss Walsingham ...   .   MRS. ABINGTON.

CHAPTER IV.

Irritability of Mrs. Abington—Benefit of Mrs. Abington—Agreement with Garrick respecting her Engagement—Correspondence with Garrick —The Stratagem—The Maid of the Oaks; Account of the Piece; The Acting—Prologue to the Maid of the Oaks—Epilogue, The British Parliament—Lines on Mrs. Abington as Lady Bab Lardoon—Further Correspondence with Garrick—The Choleric Man—Epilogue to the Choleric Man—Letters of Garrick and Mrs. Abington; mutual recrimination—King's Benefit—Measure for Measure—Bon Ton—Boswell, Johnson, and Mrs. Abington—The Sultan—A Law Case, Counsel's Opinion—Mrs. Abington Threatens to Leave the Stage; Returns however to Drury-lane—Many Plays Performed—Mrs. Abington sets up as a Woman of Fashion; the Public Press on her Style of Dress—Lines on seeing Mrs. Abington in the character of Millamant—The Rivals—The Trip to Scarborough; Description of the Play—School for Scandal; Notes of the Actors and the Comedy itself—Mrs. Abington leaves Drury-lane.

In the early part of the year 1774, we find indications of that irritability of disposition and inclination to give trouble to her employers, which afterwards displayed itself so conspicuously, and sometimes thoroughly exhausted Garrick's patience.

FRIDAY MORNING, JAN. 20TH, 1774.

Mrs. Abington sends the part of Letitia in "The Choleric Man" to Mr. Hopkins, in order to his receiving Mr. Garrick's commands as to the person he is pleased to give it in study to for the next representation of the play. Mr. Cumberland has obligingly given his consent to her resigning of the part, and Mrs. Abington flatters herself that Mr. Garrick will have the goodness and complaisance to relieve her from a character so little calculated to her very confined style of acting.

Mrs. Abington has been very ill for some days past, but would not importune Mr. Garrick with complaints, as she saw there was a necessity for exerting herself till the new tragedy was ready.

Received ten minutes before four.—W.H.

Endorsed Mrs. Abington, with the part of
    Letitia in "Choleric Man."

The editor of the "Private Correspondence of Garrick," in allusion to this letter, says "They who had the pleasure to know

Cumberland, and have witnessed his irritation and acquiescence under such provocations, will have a just notion how obligingly he consented to resign the best actress in the theatre in the getting up a new comedy. Mrs. Abington was excessively perverse even to such a manager as Garrick."

March 15th, 1774, was Mrs. Abington's benefit, when was performed "The Way of the World," Mrs. A. taking the part of Millamant, with "The Man of Quality."

Lord Foppington	DODD.
Young Fashion	PALMER.
Lovey	WESTON.
Sir T. Clumsey	HURST.
Miss Hoyden	MRS. ABINGTON.
Nurse	MRS. BRADSHAW.

In the Spring of 1774 (May 5th) the following agreement was drawn up and duly signed by Garrick and Mrs. Abington.

It is agreed this day between Mrs. Abington and Mr. Garrick, that the former shall be engaged to him and Mr. Lacy, patentees of the theatre Royal, in Drury-lane for three years from this date, or three acting seasons, at the sum of twelve pounds a week with a benefit, and sixty pounds for clothes; the above agreement to be put into articles according to the usual form.

FRANCES ABINGTON.
D. GARRICK.
For Mr. Lacy and Himself.

Getting on to September of this year, further specimens of Mrs. Abington's growing propensity to give trouble occur.

WEDNESDAY MORNING, 1774.

MRS. ABINGTON TO MR. GARRICK.

Indeed, Sir, I could not play Violante to-morrow if my happiness in the next world depended upon it, but if you order me, I will look it over, and be perfect as soon as possible. Mrs. Sullen is ready, and I am sure if you are pleased to give yourself a moment's time to reflect upon my general conduct in the theatre, you will see that I have ever made my attention to my business and my duty to you my sole object and ambition.

I am, Sir, your most humble servant,

F. ABINGTON.

MR. GARRICK TO MRS. ABINGTON.

ADELPHI, SEPT. 26TH, 1774.

Dear Madam,—As no business can be done without being explicit, I must desire to know if you choose to perform Mrs. Sullen. The part is reserved for you, and the play must be acted soon: whoever does it with Mr. Smith must do it with me —supposing that I am ever able to be the rake again. We talked a great deal last night, and, I am sorry to say it, without my having the least idea what to do in consequence of it. If "The Tender Husband" can be done with credit, I shall immediately set to work and with "The Hypocrite." I cannot create better actors than what we have, and we must both do our best with them. Could I put you upon the highest comic pinnacle, I certainly would do it; but indeed, my dear Madam, we shall not mount much if your cold counteracting discourse is to pull us back at every step. Don't imagine that the gout makes me peevish; I am talking to you in the greatest good humour; but if we don't do our best with the best we have, it is all fruit-less murmuring and inactive repining. Something too much of this. I shall write to the author of the piece to-morrow night, which I read to you. I have yet obeyed but half his commands, as he wrote the character of Lady Bab for your ladyship. I must beg of you to speak your thoughts upon that, which after I had read it to you, I promised to let him know your sentiments. I could wish, if you say anything to me of our stage business, you would send it separately from your opinion of "The Maid of the Oaks" and "Lady Bab." With your leave I could wish to enclose what you say of the last to the author.

Yours most truly,

DAVID GARRICK.

Endorsed,

"A letter to Mrs. Abington, in which her manner of doing and saying is not described amiss."

Nov. 3rd, 1774, "The Stratagem."

Archer	...	...	...	...	GARRICK.
Scrub	...	...	...	...	WESTON.
Foigard	...	...	...	...	MOODY,
Mrs. Sullen	...	...	...	...	MRS. ABINGTON.
Cherry	...	...	...	...	MISS POPE.

Nov. 5th, " The Maid of the Oaks," (never acted).

Dupely	Dodd.
Old Groveley	King.
Sir Harry Groveley	Brereton.
Hurry	Weston.
Oldworth	J. Aikin.
Painter	Moody.
Lady Bab Lardoon	Mrs. Abington.
Maria	Mrs. Baddeley.

This piece was written by Gen. Burgoyne expressly for Mrs. Abington, whose abilities had considerably excited his attention and admiration. " It was originally intended to have been in two acts, but by the advice of Garrick, and the assistance of singing, dancing, &c., it was spun out to five. It has since been reduced to two acts, in which shape it must be considered as a particularly good little Comedy—the language is very neat— the character of Lady Bab is excellent; it was admirably well acted by Mrs. Abington, to whom General Burgoyne has contrived to pay a very happy and deserved compliment, when he makes Lady Bab say " You shall see what an excellent actress I should have made, if fortune had not unluckily brought me into the world an Earl's daughter."

The plot as condensed by Genest is this :—Sir Harry is going to marry Maria, who is supposed to be an orphan brought up by Oldworth—the wedding is to be celebrated with a *fête champêtre*—Dupely and Lady Bab are invited—Dupely considers himself as quite an over-match for the women—Lady Bab is addicted to fashionable follies without being absolutely corrupted by them—she is desirous of making a fool of Dupely—for this purpose she puts on the dress of a shepherdess, which she meant to wear at the *fête*—Dupely makes love to her as Philly Nettletop of the vale—Harry enters and addresses her as Lady Bab—she laughs at Dupely—in the meantime Old Groveley arrives—he is angry with Sir Harry for marrying without his knowledge—he takes a great fancy to Maria—Oldworth discovers himself to be her father. The play was acted twenty-five times, and, though adversely criticised by some, met with a generally favourable reception.

A writer in the *Sentimental Magazine* for Nov., 1774, says, " On Saturday, the 5th of November I went to Drury-lane Play-house to see the new dramatic piece called " The Maid of Oaks." As a comedy, the critics seem universally to condemn this production, and pronounce it not only destitute of sufficient fable to support five acts, but destitute also of sufficient character to admit the possibility of any considerable plot. These sagacious gentlemen, however, should remember that the "Maid of the Oaks" is not given as a comedy. but avowedly the vehicle of a pastoral festivity, lately celebrated by several persons of the first distinction; the critics, therefore, may as well examine it by the strict rules of tragedy, as by the strict rules of comedy. The author with great propriety calls his piece a Dramatic Entertainment; and if we receive it as a Dramatic Entertainment, instead of receiving it for what it never was intended to be, we must candidly declare it one of the most elegant exhibitions that has hitherto appeared on the English theatre.

As far as the grand design could admit the introduction of fable, the author has shewn himself perfectly acquainted with the true principles of comic literature—Lady Betty Lardoon is (for its length) as capitally written as Lady Betty Modish, it abounds with wit, observation and vivacity. Mr. King's character likewise is an exquisite sketch and Weston's obviously manifests the pencil of a master. But as I have already said, the author's chief intention being to introduce an entertainment of music, dancing and scenery, he was unavoidably obliged to contract his fable, and if he has at all erred, he has erred in supposing that the plain dramatic palate of the multitude was calculated to relish a very refined dish, which is only just come into fashion with our nobility.

The attention which Mr. Garrick has shewn to the decorations of this piece, is a convincing proof that he never spares either labour or expense, where there is a likelihood of promoting the pleasure of the public. I am told that the scenery only, which has been painted on purpose for "The Maid of the Oaks," cost £1,500. This is a prodigious sum; yet it will not appear in the least extravagant to anybody who sees it. The landscapes of Claud are scarcely equal to some of the views exhibited; and if nothing beyond the bare merit of the painting was held forth to attract the town, I should not be surprised at its bringing twenty crowded houses. Mr. Garrick's care, however, has not been confined to the scenery, it has extended to the minutest object that could increase either the beauty, or the magnificence of the entertainment. The number of singers and dancers who are pastorally habited on the occasion, is incredible; and the engagement of Slingsby and Hidon, the two greatest performers in their style perhaps on earth, is a circumstance that deserves the highest approbation.

With respect to the merit of the actors in "The Maid of the

Oaks," it is, generally speaking, very considerable, and in some instances exceedingly capital. Mr. Weston was deservedly applauded for the fund of genuine pleasantry which he displayed in his part. Mr. King in the blunt, yet benevolent, proprietor of Broomstackhall, played to the hearts of the whole audience, and entered, as he always enters, with double spirit into the poet's views, where a stream of generosity is mingled with his character. Mr. Dodd in Dupely, with solely one tolerable scene, maintained his just pretensions to the favour of the town. Mr. Aickin did simple justice to Oldword; so did Mr. Brereton to Sir Harry Grovely; and in Lady Betty Lardoon it is impossible to say enough of Mrs. Abington. The quick transition of Lady Betty from the rapid playfulness of conscious beauty in high life, to the extreme of rustic simplicity, gave this great actress a fair occasion of supporting that comic superiority which she is universally allowed by the real judges of the drama; though she had little or no business but in two acts, she proved herself not more unrivalled in the walks of elegance, than in the lines of humour, and contributed essentially to the preservation of the piece. In the Epilogue particularly, such as remember the temper of the audience must acknowledge the truth of this remark; for, though the Epilogue was admirably written to follow a play highly approved, it was pregnant with evils to a play which had received any marks of even a partial disapprobation. Her manner, nevertheless, of speaking it, as well as her manner of retiring when it was spoken, converted danger into victory, and did equal honour to her good nature and her understanding.

The new Prologue spoken after the dramatic entertainment of "The Maid of the Oaks," by Mrs. Abington.

"Two Epilogues are past—and yet—absurd!
They urge, nay, push me forth to speak a third;
If you were cross indeed, and made a fuss,
It might be right to dress a pageant thus,
And hold it up, for twenty nights together,
Like Popish images to pray fair weather;
But now, the whole horizon is quite clear,
No critic goblin rides the troubled air;
No imp provokes the deep with fancy blunders,
No heathen God from high Olympus thunders.
Why should I forth?—Well, since it must be done,
What shall I say! What character put on?
Or Lady Bab, or Phill, or Abington?
For Mrs. Abington, her part I see,
Asks too much curt'sying and humility,
'Twere tedious stuff, and let me never stir,
If I am perfect in her character.

So let her pass, a creature of your own,
Born of your smiles, and murder'd with a frown :
Next, Lady Bab,—aye—there I must confess,
But what's a character without a dress ?
Stripp'd of his frock, the veriest Macaroni,
Might issue forth a very simple Tony.
For Philly then—Fly hence fantastic art,
And simple nature mold me to the part.
La ! What a power of faces here there be ?
Tho' some are mainly greasy, that I see ;
A rare assembly ! All the world is here,
In all its uses ; bread, and clothes, and beer,
Besides that pretty courting couple there ;
                    [*To the Gallery.*
Well, certain never was so rare a show !
I wonder who you be that sit below ?
Critics perhaps—Ecod it must be so.
I've heard some harm of you, and you shall know it;
That, tho' nine critics cannot make a poet,
Yet with much malice, and with little wit,
You tear the poet's children, bit by bit,
And bury the sweet babies in the pit.
Oh ! fye for shame !—but stay ye—who be those,
Like flowers upon the banks in beauteous rows !
A dainty show of tulips, belles, and beaus !
By goles, I've found you out,—sure as a gun
You are *fine Ladies !* what they call *The Ton !*
Oh ! I have heard strange stories told of you,
What, play at cards o'Sundays?—is that true ?
And when you money want,—still stranger news,
Like Macaronies, you are done by Jews !
That they examine you from top to toe !
Vat is your age, tiss propers tat I know,
Your looks are fresh and youngish, that I grant,
But dat complexion, is it health or paint ?
If I must do you, Matam—tell me all,
Vat vile lade hours, and maskerrate and pall,
Your gaming, influenzas and the doctors,
Your debts, your gaming husband, and your broctor
It cannot lasht—a Lady of the ton
For more than one year's burchase can't be done.
"Rather than this, oh ! come again those days,
When Congreve drew the world, and all its ways,
When bold intriguers try'd with winning art,
To gain their noblest prize, a woman's heart ;
When practis'd rakes wou'd lose their gold at play,
In hopes to make it up some other way :
Not so, it seems, the modern Macaroni,
He thro' the live-long night will court—your money,
Rifle your purse, and leave you when 'tis done,
To think on what was past, and sigh alone."
Shame on these wretched times, when guilty play
Makes the night hideous and deforms the day.

"When man estrang'd from nature we behold
Polluted, horrid ! with the love of gold."
When even beauty dips with erring aim
Her rosy fingers in the sordid game,
Oh ! that the voice of reason from the stage,
Could check this fatal madness of the age,
Then would the poet every wish obtain,
And Philly Nettletop not preach in vain."

N.B.—Those lines marked with inverted commas are omitted in the
speaking on account of the extraordinary length.

An Epilogue, likewise was delivered by Mrs. Abington, com-
paring the resolutions of the audience to those of the British
Parliament. She assumed with great pleasantry, the character
of the noble speaker, and put the question whether "the bill
should pass" for the author to "possess Parnass ;" which
passed in the affirmative, the "ayes having it."

EPILOGUE.

Written by Mr. GARRICK.   Spoken by Mrs. ABINGTON.

" In parliament, whene'er a question comes,
Which makes the chief look grave, and bite his thumbs,
A knowing one is sent, sly as a mouse,
To peep into the humour of the house :
I am that mouse : peeping at friends and foes,
To find which carry it—the ayes or noes.
With more than power of parliament you sit,
Despotic representatives of wit !
For in a moment, and without much pother,
You can dissolve this piece, and call another:
As 'tis no treason, let us frankly see,
In what they differ, and in what agree,
The said supreme assembly of the nation.
With this our great dramatic convocation !
Business in both oft meets with interruption :
In both, we trust, no brib'ry or corruption ;
Both proud of freedom, have a turn to riot,
And the best speaker cannot keep you quiet .
Nay, there as here he knows not how to steer him—
When order, order's drown'd in hear him, hear him !
We have, unlike to them, one constant rule,
We open doors, and choose our gall'ries full :
For a full house both send abroad their summons ;
With us together sit the lords and commons,
You ladies here have votes—debate, dispute,
There if you go ! (O fie for shame) your'e mute,
Never was heard of such a persecution,
'Tis the great blemish of the constitution !
No human laws should nature's rights abridge,
Freedom of speech ! our dearest privilege.
Ours is the wiser sex tho' deem'd the weaker ;

I'll put the question—if you choose me speaker :
Suppose me now be-wigg'd, and seated here,
I call to order ! you the chair ! the chair !
Is it your pleasure that this bill should pass—
Which grants this poet, upon Mount Parnas'
A certain spot, where never grew or corn or grass?
Is it your pleasure that this bill should pass?
You that would pass this play, say aye, and save it ;
You that say *no* would damn it—the *ayes* have it.

LINES

On Mrs. Abington being announced in Lady Bab Lardoon, in
"The Maid of the Oaks," after an absence from the stage of
two months.

" Some there have been who've trod the stage,
Who gave the fashionable rage,
    To every well-bred Belle ;
Whilst others sought, nor sought in vain,
To find the wreath of lasting fame,
    Where laugh and humour dwell.

But, born to fill the Comic round,
Thy powers the two extremes have found,
    By Taste and Nature's clue.
Hence, in thy Lady Bab, we find
The rustic and the polish'd mind,
    By turns brought out to view.

Come then, O come, dispel those fears
Thy absence gave me, ev'n to tears,
    And let us never part.
Be "fashion's glass" as heretofore,
Draw Critics, Beaus, and Belles once more,
    And charm each eye and heart !

MR. GARRICK TO MRS. ABINGTON.

ADELPHI, NOV. 9TH.

Mr. Garrick's compliments to Mrs. Abington, and has sent
her on the other side a little alteration (if she approves it, not
else) of the epilogue, where there seems to be a patch : it should,
he believes, run thus :—

" Such a persecution !
'Tis the great blemish of the constitution !
No human laws should Nature's rights abridge,
Freedom of speech, our dearest privilege ;
Our's is the wiser sex, though deemed the weaker,
I'll put the Question, if you'll cheer me Speaker.
Suppose me now be-wigged," etc.

Mrs. A. is at full liberty to adopt this alteration or not. Had
not our house overflowed last night in a quarter of an hour,

from the opening of Covent Garden had suffered much. As it was there was great room in the pit and gallery at the end of the third act.

Much joy I sincerely wish you at your success in Lady Bab. May it continue till we both are tired, you with playing the part, and I with seeing it.

  MRS. ABINGTON, 62, PALL MALL.

A month after, Garrick wrote—

          ADELPHI, DEC. 8TH.

Dear Madam—I altered the beginning of your epilogue merely for your ease and credit. I leave it wholly to your own feelings to decide what to speak or what to reject. I find the epilogue is liked, and therefore I would make it as tolerable as possible for you. I assure you, upon my word, that if you please yourself, you will please me. In my hurry I find, looking over the lines this afternoon, that I have made a false chime. I have made directed and corrected to chime, which will not do; suppose them thus :—

> Does not he know, poor soul, to be detected
> Is what you hate, and more to be corrected.

or this :—

> Does not he know, in faults to be detected
> Is what you hate, and more to be corrected.

I most sincerely wish you joy of your friend's success. The comedy will be in great vogue.

  I am, Madam, your very humble servant,

        D. GARRICK.

On Nov. 16th of this year, 1774, was performed "The Provoked Wife," Mrs. Abington playing Lady Fanciful.

Dec. 19th, "The Choleric Man," never acted. Mrs. Abington played Letitia, a part she had earlier in the year rejected, or objected to, as unsuitable.

EPILOGUE

To the New Comedy of "The Cholerick Man."

Written by Mr. GARRICK, and spoken by Mrs. ABINGTON.

> "As I'm an Artist, can my skill do better
> Than paint your pictures? for I'm much your debtor :
> I'll draw the outlines—finish at my leisure—
> A groupe like you would be a charming treasure !
> Here is my Pencil, here my Sketching-book,
> Where for this work I memorandums took ;
> I will in full, three quarters, and profile,
> Take your sweet faces, nay, your thoughts I'll steal ;

From my good friends above, their wives and doxies,
Down to Madame and Monsieur in the Boxes :
Now for it, Sirs ! I beg, from top to bottom,
You'll keep your features fix'd till I have got 'em.
First for Fine Gentlemen my fancy stretches—
They'll be more like, the slighter are the sketches :
Such unembodied form invention racks ;
Pale cheeks, dead eyes, thin bodies, and long backs— }
They would be best in shades, or virgin's wax.
To make Fine Ladies like, the toil is vain,
Unless I paint 'em o'er and o'er again :
In frost tho' not a flower its charms discloses,
They can, like hot-houses, produce their roses.
At you, Coquettes, my Pencil now takes aim !
In love's 'Change-Alley playing all the Game, }
I'll paint you Ducklings waddling out quite lame.
The Prude's most virtuous spite I'll next pourtray ;
Railing at gaming—loving private play.
Quitting the gay Bon-ton, and Wou'd-be-witty,
I come to you, my Patrons, in the City :
I like your honest, open, English looks ;
They shew too—that you well employ your cooks !
Have at you, now—Nay, Mister—pray don't stir,
Hold up your head, your fat becomes you, Sir ;
Leer with your eyes—as thus—now smirk—Well done !
Your ogling, Sir—a haunch of venison.
Some of your fickle Patriots I shall pass—
Some brittle Beings will be best on glass.
Now, Courtiers, you—Looks meant your thoughts to smother—
Hands fix'd on one thing—eyes upon another.
For Politicians I have no dark tints—
Such clouded brows are fine for wooden prints.
To distant climes if modern Jasons roam,
And bring the golden Fleece with curses home,
I'll blacken them with Indian ink—but then
My hands, like theirs, will ne'er be clean again.
Though last, not least in love, I come to you !*
And 'tis with rapture Nature's sons I view ;
With warmest tints shall grow your jolly faces,
Joy, Love, and Laughter, there have fix'd their places, }
Free from weak nerves, Bon-Ton, ennui, and foreign Graces,
I'll tire you now no more with Pencil strictures ;
I'll copy these—next week send home your Pictures.

We have now reached the year 1775, an interesting feature
connected with which is the correspondence between Mrs. Abington and Garrick, and which, perhaps more than anything else,
shews the effect of prosperity upon her character and the
exceedingly difficult task Garrick had before him in endeavouring
to please her and efficiently meet her wishes.

Between the evening in March, when Mrs. A. took her benefit,
and the 21st of the ensuing October, she seems to have been

* To the Galleries.

missing from the theatre, and from the correspondence we shall now lay before our readers, it is pretty clear that that interval was occupied in writing angry and sarcastic letters.

MRS. ABINGTON TO MR. GARRICK.

MONDAY NIGHT, MARCH 6TH, 1775.

Mr. Garrick behaves with so much unprovoked incivility to Mrs. Abington, that she is at a loss how to account for it; and her health and spirits are so much hurt by it, that she is not able to say *what* or when she can play. If he had been pleased to have given her a day's notice, she could have played her part in " The West Indian;" but it was not possible for her at three o'clock to read her part, get her clothes ready, and find a hair-dresser all by six o'clock, and that too at a time when she is in a very weak and ill state of health.

If Mr. Garrick really thinks Mrs. Abington so bad a subject as he is pleased to describe her in all the companies he goes into, she thinks his remedy is very easy, and is willing on her part to release him from so great an inconvenience as soon as he pleases; and only begs, while he is pleased to continue her in his theatre, that he will not treat her with so much harshness as he has lately done.

MR. GARRICK TO MRS. ABINGTON.

ADELPHI, MARCH 7, 1775.

Madam—Whether [it be] a consciousness of your unaccountable and unwarrantable behaviour to me, or that you have really heard of *my description of you* in all companies, I will not enquire; whatever I have said I will justify, for I always speak the truth. Is it possible for me to describe you as your note of yesterday describes yourself. You want a day's notice to perform a character you played originally, and which you have appeared in several times this season: you knew our distress yesterday almost as soon as I did, and did not plead the want of a day's notice, clothes, hair-dresser, &c., but you refused on account of your health, though you were in spirits and rehearsing a new farce. You suffered us to be obliged to another lady, of another house, to do your business, when neither our distresses, the credit of the theatre, or your own duty and justice, could have the least influence upon you. How could I give you a day's notice when I knew not of Mr. Reddish's illness but in the morning? and you were the first person I sent to between *twelve and one*, and not at *three* o'clock. It was happy for us that we found a lady, though not of our company, who had feeling for our

E

distress, and relieved us from it without requiring a day's notice, or wanting any thing but an opportunity to show her politeness. These are serious truths, Madam, and are not to be described like the lesser peccadillos of a fine lady. A little time will show that Mr. Garrick has done essential offices of kindness to Mrs. Abington, when his humanity only, and not his duty obliged him. As to your wishes of delivering me from the inconvenience of your engagement, that, I hope, will soon be another concern. My greatest comfort is, that I shall soon be delivered from the capriciousness, inconsistency, injustice, and unkindness, of those to whom I always intended the greatest good in my power.

Iam, Madam, Your most obedient servant,

D. GARRICK.

Your refusing to play this evening has obliged me, though but just recovered from a dreadful disorder, to risk a relapse.

MRS. ABINGTON TO MR. GARRICK.

TUESDAY MORNING, MARCH 7TH, 1775.

Sir,—From your not recollecting some circumstances, your letter is a misrepresentation of facts from the beginning to the end.

You are pleased to say "The West Indian" has been performed several times this season; it has really been acted but once, and that at the very beginning of the winter. You say I was well and in spirits at the rehearsal. Indeed, Sir, whoever told you so, deceived you; I was very ill, and not able to hold myself up in my chair. You say I knew the distress of the theatre at twelve o'clock. I saw very little distress, for it was plain that "The Country Girl" could have been acted from the instant that Mr. Reddish's illness was known; the design, therefore, of changing it to "The West Indian" could only be to hurt and hurry me; and if I refused, it was a good pretence for borrowing a performer to play my part, in order to give colour to the abuse that was intended for me in the papers this morning. I have, however, been too attentive to my business, and too faithful a servant both to you, Sir, and to the public, to suffer from such malice and ill nature; and if you refuse me the indulgence that is due to me for all the labour and attention I have given to the theatre, for this winter in particular, and for many years past, I must at least remember what is due to myself; and if the newspapers are to be made the vehicles of your resentment to me, I must justify myself in the best manner I can.

I am, Sir, your obedient and most humble,

F. ABINGTON.

MR. GARRICK TO MRS. ABINGTON.

ADELPHI, MARCH 7TH, 1775.

Madam,—I beg that you will indulge yourself in writing what you please and when you please. If you imagine that I in the least countenance, or am accessory to any scribbling in the papers, you are deceived. I detest all such methods of showing my resentment. I never heard of the disorder which was occasioned in "The Maid of the Oaks:" I was too ill to be troubled with it: and Mr. King, whom you have always unjustly suspected, never mentioned it to me, nor did I know of the paragraph you allude to till it was shown to me this morning. Could "The Country Girl" have been done with credit yesterday, I should not have distressed myself to have applied to you, or to have borrowed a lady from another theatre. As I will always retract the most insignificant mistake I may have made, I find by the prompter that "The West Indian" has been performed but once. May I venture, if "Braganza" cannot be performed on Thursday, to put your name in the bills for Lady Bab in "The Maid of the Oaks," or for any other part? I most sincerely assure you that I do not ask this to distress you, but to carry on the business in the best manner I am able.

I am, Madam, your most humble servant,

D. GARRICK.

Mrs. Yates has not yet sent word that she cannot play on Thursday, and I hope you may be excused. I ask the question to prevent trouble to both.

The writing peevish letters will do no business.

MRS. ABINGTON TO MR. GARRICK.

THURSDAY, TWO O'CLOCK, 1775.

Sir,—"A paragraph to say that 'The Sultan' is withdrawn "* would be a very singular and a very new object: however, as that threat is only meant in harshness and insult to me, it is neither new nor singular; and all the answer I should make to such a paragraph would be that I had withdrawn myself from the theatre, which I should most undoubtedly have done some years since, but that Mr. Garrick has so much real goodness in his nature, that no ill effects need ever be dreaded in a situation where he has the entire government.

I will endeavour, and I think it is possible to be ready by

---

* A farce really written by Bickerstaff.—Ed.

Tuesday, as I see " The Sultan," is advertised for that day ; but I shall want many little helps, particularly in the business of the dinner scene, and about my song, as I am at best a bad stick in that line as well as in most others, God knows.

I am, Sir, &c. &c.,

F. ABINGTON.

MRS. ABINGTON TO MR. GARRICK.

WEDNESDAY MORNING.

Mrs. Abington has kept her room with a fever for some days past, or she would have complained to Mr. Garrick of a letter she has received from Mr. Hopkins, dictated in the spirit of incivility and misrepresentation. He says it is written by order of Mr. Garrick, which Mrs. Abington is the more surprised at, as she is not conscious that her conduct in the theatre has deserved so much acrimony and ill humour. She apprehends that for some time past she has had enemies about Mr. Garrick, and it is to them she supposes herself indebted for the very great change in Mr. Garrick's behaviour; after all the fatigue she has undergone, and the disappointment she has experienced in respect to the business that was by agreement to be done for her this winter.

She hopes that Mr. Garrick has got some person to perform the part of " Letitia in " The Choleric Man," and in respect to the epilogue, she takes the liberty of referring him to Mr Hopkins, with whom she left a message upon that subject.

MRS. ABINGTON TO MR. GARRICK.

TUESDAY, THREE O'CLOCK.

Mrs. Abington presents her compliments to Mr. Garrick, and is very sorry to read of his indisposition ; she is very ill herself, and exceedingly hurt that he should accuse her of *want of zeal for the cause,* as she flatters herself that Mr. Garrick is fully persuaded, she has never been wanting in duty and attachment to the business of his theatre.

But she thinks she is entitled to the same degree of indulgence that is given to other performers, and hoped that Mr. Garrick would have had the goodness to let her come out in some part of stronger comic humour than that of Millamant.

She begs that he will not be angry, or treat her with harshness, as he will certainly find her a very faithful and useful subject, if he will condescend to think her worth a very little degree of attention and consideration.

She will play in "The Hypocrite" and "Bon Ton," on Saturday if he pleases, and will be ready in "The Way of the World" the beginning of the next week, but trouble him for an answer if that measure is approved.

Endorsed,
" Mrs. Abington about acting."

MRS. ABINGTON TO MR. GARRICK.

MONDAY, MAY 27TH.

Sir—I am very much indisposed, and desire to be excused when I tell you I cannot act to-morrow night. If the consideration of the salary I receive is a reason for my being called out to play to empty benches, I must beg leave to decline receiving any more pay at your office; at the same time I take the liberty of assuring you that I shall be ready and willing to stay in for the purpose of acting with you, if you think proper to call for my services, and in such case shall accept of any proportion of my salary that you may think I deserve for such attendance. I beg you will not take the trouble of writing an answer, as I am sure your spirits ought to be composed for the great business of this evening. I hope you are perfectly well, and am, with great respect, Sir,

Your most humble servant,
FRANCES ABINGTON.

MRS. ABINGTON TO MR. GARRICK.

THURSDAY, JUNE 29TH, 1775.

Sir,—I received the favour of your message by Mr. Hopkins, and have sent the farce as you was pleased to command.

I am very certain that a few of your nice touches, with a little of your fine polish, will give it that stamp of merit as must secure it a reception with the public, equal to the warmest of my expectations.

MR. GARRICK TO MRS. ABINGTON.

JULY 1ST, 1775.

Mr. Garrick presents his best compliments to Mrs. Abington, and she may depend upon his doing his best to give her piece success. Had the author vouchsafed to have communicated with Mr. G. the matter would have been better managed.

Endorsed,
" Mrs. Abington's note and my answer about her *petite* piece." This was sent by me the same day—T. B. *i. e.* Tho. Beckett, the Bookseller.

MRS. ABINGTON TO MR. GARRICK.

SOUTHAMPTON-STREET, JULY 14TH, 1775.

Sir,—I take this method of expressing my thanks for the very polite message you was pleased to send to me by Mr. Hopkins, of which, I beg leave to assure you, I am entirely sensible.

I am sorry to say I am as little read in *dramatic* as in other authors; but were I more conversant in this respect, I would not, in a theatre where Mr. Garrick is manager, take the liberty of catering for myself; I can only say, that the *parts* to which the actresses of *my time* owed their fame, are in the possession of other performers, particularly Beatrice, Mrs. Sullen, Clarinda, &c.; and of those others in which I have been most favourably received by the public, the plays are so altered by the death of actors, the giving up their parts, or other accidents, that they are no longer of use to the catalogue.

In the choice of new ones, therefore, I would certainly wish to be directed by you, nor will it be wondered at that I am anxious for your assistance in a point so very essential to my interest and reputation.

Whilst you, Sir, continue upon the stage, it will be the ambition of every performer to have their names appear with yours; I cannot, therefore, help reminding you of your intention to play Don John, and of your sometimes hinting that it was not impossible but you might appear in the character of the Copper Captain.

If such an event should at any time take place, it would gratify my utmost wishes; in the mean time, I have only to hope that your present disposition in my favour may continue, and I have nothing farther to desire in this world.

I am, Sir, your most obedient and most humble servant,

FRANCES ABINGTON.

Endorsed,
" Mrs. Abington about Pope's parts."

MRS. ABINGTON TO MR. GARRICK.

SOUTHAMPTON-STREET, NOV. 26TH, 1775.

Dear Sir, I am encouraged by the kind assurances you have favoured me with, and from a conversation I was accidentally engaged in last night with Mr. Murphy, to be a little importunate with you on a subject which has been the source of much discontent and unhappiness to me.

Mr. Murphy says his new comedy is not yet cast, and flattered me much by assuring me it was your opinion that it would be for the advantage of the piece that I should be in it as well as Mrs. Barry; however, if the character which the author very kindly intended for me is to be given to that lady, from what I remember of it, I fear that I cannot undertake any other part without more disadvantage to myself than you would choose to lay me under.

Permit me, dear Sir, to observe, that if I had been, at this time, on a more respectable footing at the theatre, I apprehend Mr. Murphy would not have thought it necessary for the interest of his play to have withdrawn his promise to me in favour of any other actress; and you will perhaps not think there is any very inexcusable vanity in this opinion, when you are told that upon his showing me the complimentary verses on Mrs. Barry, which were afterwards prefixed to "The Grecian Daughter," he was so obliging as to say that he would do as much for me if Mr. Garrick would let him—that is, (as I understood it,) if you received the play, the capital part of which he then designed for me.

It is in your power, dear Sir, I know it is, at any moment to put me on such a respectable footing with the public, and of course, with authors, that I should be thought not unequal to, nor be ill received in such light and easy characters of comedy as my talents confine me to: the part in question is one of those.

I am not insensible of Mrs. Barry's extensive merit; I know that she is singularly excellent in the pathetic: in the new comedy there is a character of that kind which might be made worth her acceptance. But I beg pardon, Sir; I have perhaps said too much on this point; the end of my application is sufficiently obvious, and I flatter myself, Sir, you will not think it unreasonable or impertinent, but favour it with your kind attention.

I am, dear Sir,

Your much obliged and very humble servant,

FRANCES ABINGTON.

MR. GARRICK TO MRS. ABINGTON.

ADELPHI, FRIDAY, NOV. 27TH, 1775.

Madam,—I am always happy to see the performers of merit, who belong to us, happy and satisfied; but if I were to make myself uneasy when they are pleased, right or wrong, to be discontented, I cannot pay them the compliment to mortify myself for nothing. After I have said this, let me be permitted to say

farther, that I never yet saw *Mrs. Abington* theatrically happy
for a week together; there is such a continual working of a
fancied interest, such a refinement of importance, and such
imaginary good and evil, continually arising in the politician's
mind, that the only best substantial security for public applause
is neglected for these shadows. That I may hear no more of
this or *that* part in Mr. Murphy's play, I now again tell you,
that every author, since my management, distributed his parts
as he thinks will be of most service to his interest, nor have I ever
interfered, or will interfere, unless I perceive that they would
propose something contrary to common sense. As I cannot
think this to be the case between Mrs. Barry and you, I must beg
leave to decline entering into the matter. I sincerely wish, for
all our sakes, that you may have a character worthy of you, as
well as Mrs. Barry. I can no more. You sometimes pay me
the compliment to say that you would do anything I should
advise; I flatter myself, if you had done so, you would not
have repented of your politeness. I never advised you to play
Ophelia, though that has been unjustly laid to my charge.
I advised you to take Maria, and was polite enough to send
you the play; you sent both the part and book back, with
incivility to me, and great injustice to yourself. Mrs. B. has
discovered what you would not, and has taken it—wisely taken
it. Remember to tell your friends that you *might* have played
Maria, but *political refinement*, the ban of all our actions, prevented you. I shall in no wise hinder Mr. Murphy from paying
you any compliments his friendship or kindness may intend
you; and if they depended upon my accepting his play, I have
done my part towards it, for it is accepted. I am sure Mr.
Murphy means you well, and thinks justly of your talents; and
I would not have you quarrel with him because his gratitude
for the favours he has received in "The Grecian Daughter"
may have made him willing to oblige Mrs. B. by another part
in his next play. Now, Madam, I have done. You wished to
play "The Scornful Lady;" I fetched an alteration of that play
from Hampton on purpose. I am very willing to do you all
the justice in my power, and I could wish you would *represent
me so* to persons *out* of the theatre, and, indeed, for your own
sake, for I always hear this tittle-tattle again, and have it
always in my power to prove that I am never influenced by
any little considerations to be unjust to Mrs. Abington or any
other performer.

I am, Madam, your most humble servant,
D. GARRICK.

I would have answered your letter last night, but I was prevented by company. A sister arrived from the country, has taken up all my time till this moment.

MRS. ABINGTON TO MR. GARRICK.

SOUTHAMPTON-STREET,

FRIDAY NIGHT, NOV. 27TH, 1775.

Sir,—Your letter is very cross, and such a one as I had no apprehension I should provoke by what I intended as a respectful application for your favour and protection.

Among the long train of accusations you unkindly urge against me, give me leave to exculpate myself of one only—I mean the charge of incivility to you in returning the part of Maria in "The Duel." When you recommended that part to me, Mr. Hopkins gave me the play, and desired I would return it in the morning; it was then late at night. I gave it a hasty reading, and returned it accordingly, telling him I could not see much in the part; however, I would play it if Mr. Garrick desired or insisted upon it. The part was never sent me; the charge, therefore, of my sending it back with incivility to you, must certainly have arisen from some misinformation.

There is a coldness, a severity, in your letter, which at this time adds greatly to the affliction of your distressed humble servant,

FRANCES ABINGTON.

MRS. ABINGTON TO MR. GARRICK.

Mrs. Abington has great complaints to make to Mr. Garrick respecting a servant in his theatre for very impertinently writing against her in the newspapers last night, only for begging leave to sit in the prompter's box to see one act of a play on a night that she was to perform in "Bon Ton;" when her head was dressed, ready to begin the farce, which was the reason she could not so conveniently go to any other part of the house.

MRS. ABINGTON TO MR. GARRICK.

THURSDAY, TWELVE O'CLOCK.

Sir,—The servant has brought me word that Mr. Garrick is very angry at my not attending rehearsal this morning.

I do not believe him. I am sure Mr. Garrick did not expect I could be able to go out this morning, after the labour I have very willingly gone through for three nights past. I am ill to death, and really not able to stand; I cannot, therefore, think

that much apology for my staying away is necessary, when the
cause is so well known.

I am not perfect in the part in "The Sultan," and have been
put out of humour with it by being told that Mr. Andrews talks
of the farce at the coffee-houses as the work of Mr. Kelly, which
is so far from being a fact, that, I declare to God, Mr. Kelly
has never so much as seen it; and the report can only be meant
to bring popular prejudice against it. I most sincerely wish
that Mr. Andrew's farce was out, and had received that approbation which there can be no doubt of its meriting; he would
then perhaps not take the trouble of considering about who
was the author of "The Sultan,"* or at least not give it to a
gentleman who has never seen a line of it.

I have once more to hope that Mr. Garrick will let it come
out after Christmas, as the present powerful run of "Bon Ton,"
makes it very hard upon me, in the idea of being constantly
upon the stage in two farces, one of which is like something
dropped from the clouds, and only made its appearance at the
benefits last year, or I should not have interested myself
about the other, knowing the impossibility of my attempting
that line of business while I am necessarily engaged in so many
plays.

I am, sir, &c.,

F. ABINGTON.

MRS. ABINGTON TO MR. GARRICK.

SUNDAY MORNING, TEN O'CLOCK.

Mrs. Abington was surprised at receiving a message from Mr.
Garrick last night respecting the part of Araminta, in "The
School for Lovers," as she had flattered herself that he under-
stood her reasons for wishing to resign that character; if he
does not, she refers him to a note which she wrote to Mr.
Bensley on Friday morning.

Mrs. Abington takes leave to acquaint Mr. Garrick that she
is very ill, and has been so for some days; though she was not
wiling to trouble him with an account of her indisposition; nor
would she wish to be excused from the business of the theatre
when she is at all able to put on her clothes, or walk upon the
stage.

She is greatly surprised to see "The Hypocrite" advertised
for Wednesday, and begs it may not be continued with *her name*
in it, as she certainly cannot play in it on Wednesday; indeed,
if she was well enough to perform so long a part as that of

* " It was really Bickerstaff's "—Editor of Garrick's Letters.

Charlotte, Mr. Garrick knows that the play will not bring *half a house*, and it would be very hard that she should be obliged to play to empty benches* merely to gratify Mr. Garrick's present resentment to her. Mrs. Abington told Mr. Garrick that she would play in any farce after *that* play that might be supposed to have strength enough to help to fill the house; but his answer was, that *he was Manager*. She understands perfectly well his power as a manager; and is very willing to submit to it, when it is not exercised in endeavours to destroy her health, her peace of mind, and her credit with the public.

She is willing to act in any plays that are ready, and can be creditably performed: if the plays are *not ready*, and that Mr. Garrick has no occasion for Mrs. Abington, she repeats the requests she made last year, that he will give her up her agreement, and not make "The Morning Post" the vehicle of his resentment.

On the 18th of March, 1775, was acted at Drury-lane for King's benefit, "Measure for Measure," (not acted for 16 years) and an excellent little comedy by Garrick, called "Bon Ton," in three acts. In this latter piece, Mrs. Abington played the part of Miss Tittup. The acting throughout is described as particularly good.

Garrick, in a short advertisement says, "This little drama was brought out last season for the benefit of Mr. King, as a token of regard for one, who during a long engagement, was never known, unless confined by real illness, to disappoint the public, or distress the managers."

Genest says: The prologue by Colman was so good and so well delivered, that King always spoke it till he left the stage.

March 27th, Mrs. Abington's benefit, when was performed "The Hypocrite" and "Bon Ton," now reduced to two acts.

In allusion to this benefit, we find the following interesting particulars in Boswell's Life of Johnson.

On Monday, March 27th (1775), I breakfasted with him (Johnson), at Mrs. Strahan's. He told us that he was engaged to go that evening to Mrs. Abington's benefit. She was visiting

---

* When I remember this lady's excellence, I am ashamed of her perverse dishonest arts. If the play of itself will fill a house, she will act in it; if it will not, she cannot act to *empty benches:* she will add attraction to strength, but always refuse it to weakness. The power of a manager indeed! what is it to an actress of powerful talent, backed by half the women of fashion in the metropolis?—Editor of Garrick correspondence.

some ladies whom I was visiting and begged that I would come to her benefit. I told her I could not hear ; but she insisted so much on my coming, that it would have been brutal to have refused her. This was a speech quite characteristical. He loved to bring forward his having been in the gay circles of life, and he was perhaps a little vain of the solicitations of this elegant and fashionable actress. I met him at Drury-lane play-house in the evening. Sir Joshua Reynolds, at Mrs. Abington's request, had promised to bring a body of wits to her benefit ; and having secured forty places in the front boxes, had done me the honour to put me in the group. Johnson sat on the seat directly behind me, and as he could neither see nor hear at such a distance from the stage, he was wrapped up in grave abstraction, and seemed quite a cloud amidst all the sunshine of glitter and gaiety. I wondered at his patience in sitting out a play of five acts and a farce of two. He said very little ; but after the prologue to " Bon Ton " had been spoken, which he could hear pretty well from the more slow and distinct utterance, he talked on prologue writing, and observed, " Dryden has written pro-logues superior to any that David Garrick has written, but David Garrick has written more good prologues than Dryden has done. It is wonderful that he has been able to write such a variety of them."

On Friday, 31st March, I supped with him and some friends at a tavern. One of the company attempted, with too much forwardness, to rally him on his late appearance at the theatre ; but had reason to repent of his temerity. " Why, sir, did you go to Mrs. Abington's benefit ? Did you see ? " Johnson : " No, sir." " Did you hear ? " Johnson : " No, sir." " Why then, sir, did you go ? " Johnson : " Because, sir, she is a favourite of the public, and when the public cares a thousandth part for you that it does for her, I will go to your benefit too."

On Saturday, April 8th, I dined with him at Mr. Thrale's, where we met the Irish Dr. Campbell. Johnson had supped the night before at Mrs. Abington's with some fashionable people whom he named, and he seemed much pleased with having made one in so elegant a circle. Nor did he omit to pique his mistress a little with jealousy of her housewifery ; for he said with a smile, " Mrs. Abington's jelly, my dear lady, was better than yours."

Oct. 21st, " Conscious Lovers," Mrs. Abington as Phillis. (first appearance since March 27th.) Whether her absence was caused by illness or irritability of temper, it is impossible to say, some are of opinion that it was through illness.

Oct. 31st, "The Provoked Wife."

Sir John Brute	GARRICK.	
Constant	BRERETON (1st time.)	
Heartfree	BENSLEY (1st time.)	
Razor	BADDELEY.	
Col. Bully	VERNON.	
Lady Fanciful	MRS. ABINGTON.	
Lady Brute	MISS YOUNGE.	
Belinda	MRS. GREVILLE.	
Mademoiselle	MRS. BRADSHAW.	

Nov. 6th, "Much Ado about Nothing."

Benedick	GARRICK.
Claudio	BRERETON (1st time.)
Beatrice	MRS. ABINGTON (1st time.)

Dec. 1st, "The Stratagem."

Archer	GARRICK.
Scrub	YATES.
Mrs. Sullen	MRS. ABINGTON.
Cherry	MISS JARRATT.

Dec. 12th, Richard the III., with, never acted, "The Sultan, or a Peep in the Seraglio."

Solyman the Great	PALMER.
Osmyn	BANNISTER.
Roxalana	MRS. ABINGTON.
Elmira	MRS. KING.
Ismena	MRS. WRIGHTEN.

" The Sultan " had been very much enamoured of Elmira, but his love had cooled—Osmyn (chief of the Eunuchs) complains to the Sultan that Roxalana (an English slave) is ungovernable— the Sultan represents to her the impropriety of her conduct — she treats his remonstrance with lenity—he falls in love with her—she at last gains such an influence over him, that he makes her his wife."

Mrs. Abington gave to the volatile Roxalana that elegance and grace which has so long distinguished her character. She was very much applauded, and the audience testified their approbation of the piece in the strongest terms.

The year 1776 brought with it a return of the paper war between Mrs. Abington and Garrick, which we have already noticed ; the following letters will show that things instead of getting better began to assume a more serious character in spite of all outward appearances of cordiality.

Before giving the 1776 correspondence however, we insert the following letter, written in December, 1775, (dated the 5th), which is evidently connected with their disputes, though the special particulars appear unknown.

Mr. Garrick to Mrs. Abington.

Dec. 5th, 1775.

Madam,—I beg that you will keep Mr. Andrews' note, it is a justification to you; and had he been guilty of the least endeavour to prejudice "The Sultan," I would never have spoken to him again; be assured I have done my utmost for the piece, and had it not come out till Tuesday or Wednesday, we should, as well as you, have been great sufferers; I shall take care that you are kept from playing, till you appear in the new piece; we will settle business of the table and guitar when we meet. I cannot attend you to-morrow, because I have a long and laborious part. On Saturday, I shall attend, and settle the whole.

I took care that Mrs. Wrighten should not have a gay song, nor do I understand it will in the least interfere with you—and don't be uneasy, a natural, gay chansonette song, with natural ease and pleasantry, will be heard with pleasure, after the first embroidered air of a Farinelli. I believe an Emperor of the Turks was never seen before. Mr. Palmer will make his first appearance in "The Sultan." If you would have Mr. Shaw oblige you most completely, a few half-guineas would be well bestowed, to have him home to your house, and settle the song and accompaniments with you. Don't starve your business for trifles. I have done my utmost for the piece, and it will be most splendid in scenery and dresses.

Yours very *truly*, when
You are not *unruly*,
D. Garrick.

Mrs. Abington to Mr. Hopkins.

Tuesday, Three o'clock, Jan. 30th, 1776.

Sir—You will be pleased to let the manager know that I am ill (though I thank God I have not lost the use of my limbs, as he has been pleased to tell the public), but I am too ill to attempt to perform to-morrow night. My friends will take an opportunity of thanking Mr. Garrick for his humanity and civility to me, which you will have the goodness to tell him, and that I am his

Most humble servant,
F. Abington.

Endorsed by Hopkins,
" Received this letter ten minutes before 5."

MR. HOPKINS TO MRS. ABINGTON.

TUESDAY NIGHT, JAN. 30TH, 1776.

Madam—I sent your letter to Mr. Garrick, who ordered me to inform you that he told no more than your servant delivered, and that he will both answer your letter and your friends at a proper time.

As to the part of Lady Fanciful, both Mr. Garrick and myself have been informed that you said you never intended to perform it again.

I am, Madam, your most humble servant,

WILLIAM HOPKINS.

CASE.—DRURY-LANE.

LINCOLN'S-INN, MARCH 1ST, 1776.

Mrs. Abington is engaged as a performer for the season at a salary and a benefit night. Benefits are generally fixed according to the rank of the performer, and that rank is determined by the rate of salary. The highest salary has the first choice of the day, and so on: Mrs. Abington stands in the fourth degree of eminence; Miss Younge, the next.

About a fortnight ago, when the benefits were fixing, Mrs. Abington had the choice of Saturday, the 16th of March, or Monday, the 18th, for her benefit. She had objections to both: Saturday was Opera-night; Monday degraded her, for she then must give precedence to Miss Younge. After weighing these important points, rank and precedence prevailed over interest; *she chose Saturday the 16th*, and Monday was given to Miss Younge. The next day, interest seemed to preponderate, and she rather wished for Monday; but this night being engaged, and not to be had, she gave out that the managers refused to give her any night for a benefit, and she has hitherto declined to advertise or make any preparations for the 16th of March.

The Managers are somewhat distressed by this untoward conduct, though they are not concerned in point of interest; but should she not prepare for that night, there will be no performance; the consequence.

They have thought of giving her a notice to the following purport:—

"I am directed by the managers to acquaint you that, conformable to your choice of Saturday, the 16th of March, for your benefit, that day was immediately allotted, and is kept for the purpose; and you will consequently name your play, that it may be got ready, and other matters prepared in proper time.

It may be right to inform you that, in consequence of your

choice of that day, all others have been settled and fixed for the other subsequent performers, and that there is no other day vacant till Easter."

And if she persists in her stubbornness till a few days before the 16th of March, then to give her notice, that a play will be performed in which she has a part, and which will be appropriated for her benefit. Or, ought the managers to let the house be shut up, and no play be performed? Or, will this conduct of her's be deemed a waiver of her benefit at night?

COUNSEL'S OPINION.

" I think the managers should send a person not interested in the house to inform her, that the managers, observing she has made no preparations for her benefit, are desirous to know whether she intends to take that night or not, as they wish to prevent a disapointment to the town, by giving a play that night if she declines her benefit. This will produce an immediate answer; whereas a notice may keep the managers in suspense. If she declines a benefit that night, the managers may give a play on their own account, without any danger of being responsible to her for the profits. It may be thought candid on the part of the managers to make her an offer of any unappointed night; declaring they do it not from any obligation thay conceive themselves under, but to convince her they have no design to take advantage of her refusal to accept of her benefit as a waiver of her right to one, which they apprehend it to be; if she refuses this offer, which is probable, then 1 think she will have no colour to claim a benefit."

JA. WALLACE.

MRS. ABINGTON TO MR. GARRICK.

LEICESTER-FIELDS, MARCH 4TH, 1776.

Sir,—As it has been for some time my fixed determination to quit the stage at the conclusion of the present season and not return to it again, I thankfully accept your very obliging intention to play for my benefit in May; you will therefore please to dispose of Saturday the 16th inst. in any manner most agreeable to yourself,

I am, Sir,

Your very much obliged and most humble servant,

FRANCES ABINGTON.

" The above is a true copy of the letter, examined word by word, of that worst of bad women Mrs. Abington, to ask my playing for her benefit, and why?—

Endorsed,

" A copy of Mother Abington's letter
about leaving the stage."

Garrick's note at the foot of the above letter shews how exasperated he felt at Mrs. A——'s conduct and her pretence that he had offered to play for her at her benefit; however he sent the following reply:—

MR. GARRICK TO MRS. ABINGTON.

MARCH 7TH, 1776.

Madam,—At my return from the country, I found your letter upon my table. I read it with great surprise, and can yet scarce believe that you are in earnest. It would perhaps be as vain as impertinent in me to caution you against being too rash in determining upon so serious a matter. My reasons for quitting the stage are many, and too strong to be withstood; you can have none but will be easily conquered by your inclination. It will therefore be worth your while to consider seriously; and if you have the least reason to repent of your late determination, the best night for a benefit, which is the last night of acting before the holidays, and which the proprietors have purchased, is at your service. If you are still absolutely resolved to quit the stage for ever, I will certainly, in May, do for Mrs. Abington what I have done for others who have made the same resolution.

I am, Madam,
Your most humble servant,
D. GARRICK.

Endorsed,
"Mrs. Abington's letter, dated March 4th, and my answer to it, sent by Ralph, 7th do., 1776."

MRS. ABINGTON TO MR. GARRICK.

LEICESTER SQUARE, APRIL 7TH, 1776.

Sir,—Upon reading the paragraph which you were pleased to send me yesterday, two objections immediately started to me. I thought it might carry an air of arrogance, and be liable to expose me to censure, as making myself of too much importance with the public: and next, the style might be thought rather abrupt and impertinent. I wish for nothing more than to retire in peace, without any pretensions to that *éclat* which must necessarily attend *your* retreat.

Mr. Lodge assures me that you were perfectly satisfied with the written declaration I sent you; and that you were so far from requiring any further condition, as to declare you were ready to play for my benefit, even though my name should not be announced in the bills.

F

Mr. Lodge waited on you a second time, to acquaint you that I thankfully accepted of your offer to play for me:—and I confidently concluded, from the unfettered generosity of the above declaration, that this business would not be farther embarrassed by advertisements, or any other unnecessary conditions.

       I am, Sir, your humble servant,

                           FRANCES ABINGTON.

     Endorsed,
" A fal-lal from Mrs. Abington."

MR. GARRICK TO MR. LODGE.

HAMPTON, EASTER MONDAY, 1776.

Sir,—If I am not mistaken, I have received a letter written by you, and signed by Mrs. Abington. Though this a little carries an air of ill-will to correspond with me by her solicitor; yet, as you are a gentleman, I shall rather think she does me a favour than an incivility.

Upon my word, I cannot conceive what fetters I have put on my generosity by any advertisement I have sent her; and if you will be pleased to unchain the lady (though she is apt to behave a little unruly to me,) I shall be much obliged to you: indeed, Sir, without a figure, I most sincerely am at a loss to guess her meaning. If she does not choose to advertise as Mrs. Pritchard and Mrs. Clive did, pray let us have no more trouble about the matter, but let her please herself; if she has any more to say, or to unsay, about this business, I shall be in town on Wednesday morning, and a note from you shall settle it with me at least.

                " Varium et mutabile semper."

Be assured that I am quite satisfied with the declaration she has given me of her quitting the stage, and I am ready to fulfil my part of the agreement on the 7th of May; therefore I hope that it will be impossible for the most refined and active imagination to raise more doubts: though if they should give me an opportunity of seeing you, I shall certainly be a gainer, for I feel myself at this moment better for your recommendation of Dr. Miersbach.

     I am, Sir, your much obliged humble servant,

                              D. GARRICK.

I have the gout in my hand, and must send you this scrawl.

Jan. 27th, 1776, "The Discovery" performed (not acted for twelve years).

Sir Anthony Branville	GARRICK.
Lord Medway	BENSLEY.
Sir Harry Flutter	DODD.
Col. Medway	BRERETON.
Lady Flutter	MRS. ABINGTON.
Mrs. Knightly	MRS. KING.
Lady Medway	MRS. HOPKINS.
Miss Richly	MISS HOPKINS.
Louisa Medway	MISS P. HOPKINS.

On this revival Garrick was the only original performer.

March 12th, for King's Benefit, "Woman's a Riddle" (not acted for ten years).

Sir Amorous Vainwit	KING.
Courtmell	SMITH.
Col. Manley	REDDISH.
Aspin	YATES.
Vulture	MOODY.
Miranda	MRS. ABINGTON.
Lady Outside	MISS YOUNGE.
Clarinda	MISS HOPKINS.

All the pit but three rows turned into boxes.

March 20th, Yates's benefit, "The Way to Keep Him," with Mrs. Abington as Widow Belmour.

April 10th, Palmer's benefit, "Twelfth Night," with Mrs. Abington as Olivia.

May 7th, Mrs. Abington's benefit, "The Stratagem," when Garrick played Archer for the last time, Mrs. A. playing Mrs. Sullen.

May 23rd, "The Suspicious Husband," Mrs. Abington as Clorinda, 1st time.

"A few weeks after her benefit, it was announced, upon undoubted authority that she had taken an hotel in Paris, which was fitting up in a superior style, for the reception of the English nobility of both sexes, on their travels; and another week had scarcely passed, before it was stated that she had given up going to France, and meant at the close of the year to retire into Wales for the remainder of her life; but the next season she was

at her old post at Drury-lane.   The following lines appeared on
the 18th October, 1776 :—

> " Scarce had our tears forgot to flow,
>   By Garrick's loss inspired.
> When Fame, to moralize the blow,
>   Said, " Abington's retired."
> Gloom'd with the news, Thalia mourn'd—
>   The Graces join'd her train ;
> And nought but sighs, for sighs return'd,
>   Were heard at Drury Lane.
> But see, 'tis false ! in Nature's style
>   She comes by Fancy graced ;
> Again gives Comedy her *smile*,
>   And fashion all her taste."

At this period she set up her carriage ; which, as actresses'
carriages were not then so common as they have been of later
days, gave the papers an opportunity for scandal. A few
specimens of journalistic criticisms will be sufficient to show
that her style of dress was at this time the theme of admiration.

" Mrs. Abington's dress boasted that elegant simplicity, for
which she has so long been considered as the Priestess of
Fashion."

" Mrs. Abington having long been considered in the *beau-monde*
as a leading example in dress, her gown on Saturday night was
of white lutestring, made close to her shape, sleeves to the
wrist, and a long train ; her hair was dressed very far back
on the sides with curls below, and not high above, nor did she
wear one of those tremendous hair frizzed peaks, which of late
have disguised the ladies,—so probably they will no more appear
as unicorns with a horn issuing from their foreheads."

" Mrs. Abington is the harbinger of the reigning fashion for the
season—a very beautiful style of petticoat of Persian origin
is among the last importations of this admired actress."

" Mrs. Abington, the pattern of fashion, has fallen into the
absurdity of wearing red powder: her influence on the *ton* is
too well known—let her at once deviate from this unnatural
French custom, or if she is determined to continue a *red head*,
let her frizeur throw a little brick-dust on her arches.   (Eye-
brows.)"

In an Italian Journal, of 1786 :—

Mrs. Abington.—" Her figure is of the tallest of that order

which rises above the middle size; her face naturally comic and vivacious, but yet so educated in the habits of polite life, as to render it difficult to delineate. Whether her *forte* lies in the performance of "Women of Fashion" or "Soubrettes,"in both she is excellent, and the alternate display of both constitutes that powerful attraction which she holds on the stage." (*New Monthly Magazine*, for 1838.)

November 19th, 1776, We find Mrs. Abington again at Drury-lane, playing Letitia in the "Old Batchelor." (Not acted for sixteen years.)

● November 29th,"Love for Love," Miss Prue by Mrs. Abington.

December 31st, "The Way of the World."

Mirabell	SMITH.
Fainall	REDDISH.
Witwou'd	KING.
Sir Witful Witwou'd	YATES.
Petulant	BADDELEY.
Waitwell	PARSONS.
Millamant	MRS. ABINGTON.
Lady Wishfort	MRS. HOPKINS.
Mrs. Marwood	MISS SHERRY.
Foible	MISS POPE.
Mrs. Fainall	MRS. GREVILLE.

IMPROMPTU.

On seeing Mrs. Abington in the character of Millamant.

" Long had Beauty and Fashion, by argument try'd
Which did most for the sex !—Who was the best guide !
The one talk'd of " natural roses and lilies,"
And quoted her Chloes, her Patties and Phillis.
The other as loudly insisted that " Nature
Without her was nought, but a poor awkward creature :
That Beauty, mere Beauty, but little avails ;
,Twas just like a ship, without rigging or sails "
At length after years spent in proving and jangling,
Without any victory gain'd by their wrangling,
They settled it so, (and each was contented)
That both by One Deputy be represented.
This treaty no sooner was published aloud,
Than Abington ! Abington ! echoed the crowd.
The Goddesses bow'd to so solemn a voice,
And Taste, as High Priestess, confirmed the choice."

January 16th, 1777, "The Rivals," never acted there.

Lydia Languish   ...   .   MRS. ABINGTON.

February 24th, "The Trip to Scarborough," altered from Vanburgh.

Lord Foppington	DODD.
Loveless	SMITH.
Young Fashion	REDDISH.
Sir Tunbelly Clumsy	MOODY.
Col. Townley	BRERETON.
Lovy	BADDELEY.
Probe	PARSONS.
BERINTHIA	MRS. YATES.
Amanda	MRS. ROBINSON.
Miss Hoyden	MRS. ABINGTON.

"When this play was first acted the newspapers abused it; and in 1779 Sheridan was asked in print, if he did not consider this comedy as an illustration of what Dangle says in "The Critic," that "Vanburgh and Congreve are obliged to undergo a bungling reformation." The editor of the *B. D.* likewise censures it severely, but does not condescend to enter into particulars. In spite of all that has been said, it may confidently be affirmed that we have very few such good alterations of old plays as this. Sheridan has retained everything in the original that was worth retaining, has omitted what was exceptionable, and has improved it by what he has added—particularly the first scene in the fifth act, which concludes that part of the plot which concerns Loveless, &c., much better than it is concluded in the "Relapse." It must be confessed that it is highly improbable (as Collier observed originally), that Sir Tunbelly and Lord Foppington should negotiate a match through the mediation of such a person as Coupler: this however is a fault radically inherent in the piece; and it certainly lies at Vanburgh's door and not at Sheridan's. Sheridan makes Loveless say, "It would surely be a pity to exclude the productions of some of our best writers for want of a little wholesome pruning; which might be effected by any one who possessed modesty enough to believe that we should preserve all we can of our deceased authors, at least till they are outdone by the living ones." (Genest.)

We now reach May 8th, when was acted for the first time that now world-renowned piece of Sheridan's, "The School for Scandal," and in which Mrs. Abington played a part that gave her the name under which she is sometimes mentioned by dramatic biographers. The cast stood thus :

Sir Peter Teazle	KING.
Charles Surface	SMITH.
Joseph Surface	PALMER.
Sir Oliver Surface	YATES.
Crabtree	PARSONS.
Sir Benjamin Backbite... ...	DODD.
Moses	BADDELEY.
Trip	LAMASH.
Snake	PACKER.
Rowley	J. AIKIN.
Careless	FARREN.
Sir Harry Bumper	GAWDRY.
Lady Teazle	MRS. ABINGTON.
Mrs. Candour	MISS POPE.
Lady Sneerwell	MISS SHERRY.
Maria	MISS P. HOPKINS.

The play is described in the journals and magazines of the day as having been admirably acted, all the actors doing great justice to their respective characters, while Mrs. Abington, in Lady Teazle, gave a fresh proof of her easy elegant manner, and her unrivalled vivacity. Fifty years after, it was said, "this comedy was so admirably acted, that though it has continued on the acting-list at Drury-lane, from that time to this, and been several times represented at Covent Garden and the Haymarket, yet no new performer has ever appeared in any one of the principal characters, that was not inferior to the person who acted it originally." (Genest.)

Walpole writes of Mrs. Abington (letter to R. Jephson, Esq., July, 1777) :—

"To my great astonishment there were more parts performed admirably in "The School for Scandal" than I almost ever saw in any play. Mrs. Abington was equal to the first of her profession, Yates (the husband), Parsons, Miss Pope, and Palmer, all shone. It seemed a marvellous resurrection of the stage. Indeed, the play had as much merit as the actors. I have seen no comedy that comes near it since "The Provoked Husband."

It was evidently the acting that charmed Walpole, for he considerably moderates his transports in subsequent letters written after he had read the play, in them he candidly admits that he found it to contain far less than he had anticipated.

So far as the performance was concerned there seemed little
to find fault with beyond the fact that the Lady Teazle of Mrs.
Abington was wanting in youthfulness, she was in fact, then but
a very few years younger than King, who played Sir Peter.
Charmed, however, by the acting, this defect escaped the notice
of the public, or became a matter of comparative indifference in
the face of such an undeniable exhibition of talent. In addition
these two seemed peculiarly adapted to each other in their
performances, and it is said that "they each lost nearly half their
soul in their separation." King evidently admired her playing
exceedingly, for he said of her delivery, "every word stabbed."

Some years after the introduction of this comedy it was
proposed to change the character of Lady Teazle somewhat,
exhibiting her rather as a country girl than a woman of fashion.
It will be remembered she is described in the play as "the
daughter of a plain country squire, sitting at her tambour frame,
in a pretty figured linen gown, with a bunch of keys at her side;
her hair combed smooth over a roll, and her apartment hung
round with fruits in worsted of her own working." In this
respect Mrs. Jordan used to play the part, but however well she
did it, it was universally allowed that Mrs. Abington, especially
in the screen scene, was superior, and it has never been disputed
that the latter actress "met with the full approval of Sheridan
and the playgoing public." The part was afterwards played by
Miss Farren with considerable success, but the recollection of
Mrs. Abington still lingered in the public mind, and Boaden
writes, "I found the younger part of the critical world little
aware how much Lady Teazle lost in being transferred to Miss
Farren. I am perfectly satisfied that Miss Farren, in comedy,
never approached Mrs. Abington nearer than Mrs. Esten did
Mrs. Siddons in tragedy."

"The dialogue of this comedy is easy and witty. It abounds
with strokes of pointed satire, and a rich vein of humour
pervades the whole, rendering it equally interesting and entertaining. The fable is well conducted, and the incidents are
managed with great judgment. There hardly ever was a
better dramatic situation than that which occurs in the fourth
act, where Sir Peter discovers Lady Teazle in Joseph Surface's
study. The two characters of the brothers are finely contrasted,
and those of the Scandal Club well imagined; the circumstances
also of adding a duel to the report of the discovery made by
Sir Peter, and making Snake beg, that his having once, in his
life, done a good action might be kept a profound secret, as he
had nothing to depend on but the infamy of his character, are

highly comic, and perfectly in nature. Upon the whole, "The School for Scandal" justifies the very great and cordial reception it met with ; it certainly is a good comedy, and we should not at all wonder if it becomes as great a favourite as the "Duenna," to which it is infinitely superior in point of sense, satire and moral."

The prologue which was well spoken by Mr. King, is the production of David Garrick, Esq. With great pleasantry it adverted to the title of the play, and shot an arrow of pointed satire at the too general proneness to detraction observable in our daily and evening papers.

In the epilogue, (which was of Mr. Coleman's writing) Mrs. Abington humourously lamented her having, as the reformed Lady Teazle, consented to quit the town, and its fashionable pleasures, for retirement and a country life. (*Universal Magazine*, 1777.)

December 4th, 1777, was acted "The Chances," Mrs. Abington as usual playing 2nd Constantia.

April 9th, 1778, for Miss Pope's benefit, "Confederacy" (not acted eight years). Corinna by Mrs. Abington.

April 19th, 1779, for the benefit of Hopkins, Prompter, and Mrs. Hopkins, "The Double Gallant," Mrs. Abington as Lady Sadlife.

Sept. 28th, "The Stratagem," Mrs. Abington as Mrs. Sullen.

Nov. 11th, "The Hypocrite," Mrs. Abington as Charlotte.

Dec. 2nd, Never-acted "Times," Mrs. Abington as Lady Mary Woodley.

April 1st, 1780, Bensley's benefit, "The Suspicious Husband," Mrs. Abington as Clarinda.

Jan. 21st, 1782, "Maid of the Oaks," Mrs. Abington as Lady Bab Lardoon.

March 18th, Smith's benefit, "The Way to Keep Him," Mrs. Abington as Widow Belmour.

Sep. 26th, Miss Farren acted Lady Teazle, first time. "Mrs. Abington left Drury-lane at the close of the preceding season ; for which Miss Farren was greatly obliged to her, as in consequence of that circumstance she came in for all the first-rate characters in comedy, and played little or no more tragedy." (Genest.)

CHAPTER V.

First appearance at Covent Garden, her Address—Way of the World —All in the Wrong—Capricious Lady—Maid of Oaks at C. G.—Careless Husband—Rule a Wife—Address at close of Season— Hypocrite—Way to Keep Him—Much Ado—Suspicious Husband—Beaux Stratagem— Double Gallant—Mrs. A. as Scrub, her disgrace therein—The West Indian—Conscious Lovers—Visit to Ireland, Profitable and Successful Engagement—Various Plays at C.G.—Absence from the Stage between 1790 and 1797—Plays for Charity in June, 1797—Return to Stage in October—Last Appearance on the Stage—Death—Tributes to her memory.

Nov. 29th, 1782, Mrs. Abington made her first appearance at Covent Garden as Lady Flutter in "The Discovery," never before acted there.

Between the first and second acts of the play, this accomplished actress came forward and was immediately saluted by a thundering applause from every part of the theatre; all hands were engaged, from the goddesses in the boxes to the gods in the upper regions. With some difficulty the tumult at length subsided, and Mrs. Abington then addressed her benefactors in a very elegant poetical *morçeau*, the purport of which was to express her sense of gratitude to the public for their goodness and partiality to her, and to request a continuation of their favours, which she considered the pride and happiness of her life.

When Mrs. Abington had finished this address, the audience honoured her a second time with a congratulatory welcome as loud, and of as long continuance as the former. Her dress was simple, but perfectly characteristic; the train and petticoat were of white and silver stuff; the body and sash of a dark carmelite satin, with short white sleeves.

MRS. ABINGTON'S ADDRESS.

"Oft have I come, ambassadress in state,
From some poor author, trembling for his fate—
Oft has a generous public heard my pray'r,
And shook, with vast applause, the troubled air—
Then why should I—a creature of your own—
Born of your smiles, and murder'd by your frown,
On this occasion fear your hearts can harden,
Tho' a noviciate now at Covent Garden.
  How oft in life thro' various scenes we range,
Yet still the heart's insensible of change;

True to its point, it looks to that alone,
And thus converts all places to its home.
So to no spot the mimic art's confin'd,
It lives an active principle of mind—
Or here, or there, my business still's the same,
Folly and Affection are my game.
    Whether the Hoyden, rough from Congreve's lays,
Unknowing in French manners, or French phrase ;
Who, conscious of no crime in speaking plain,
Will bawl out *Smock* for *Chemise de la Reine.*
    Or modish Prudes, whose visions thro' her fan ;
Who censures—shuns—yet loves that monster—man.
    Or yet the brisk Coquette, whose spreading sail
Courts every wind that can bring in a male.
    In short, good folks, tho' I have chang'd my school,
Alike you'll find me here to play the fool.
But when bright beauty, such as beams around,
With female dignity, and graces crown'd,
Thus group'd appear, our art seems at a stand,
Or we but copy with a trembling hand—
Yet if for fame or fortune we'd pursue,
'Tis to attempt originals like you.
    Now let me take a peep into the Pit—
Are there none here mistaking spleen for wit ;
Or who, deep read in Aristotle's case,
Might say, she has broken unity of place ?
And thus, by critic logic, make it plain,
That Covent Garden is not Drury-Lane.
    If such there be, who thus by measure scan,
Against his *Rule*—I parry with my fan—
An instrument, presented by the Graces,
To bear me harmless from such Gorgon faces,
    Yet let me look again—avaunt my fear,
I see no Gorgons 'midst my patrons here.
    To you, great gods, I make my last appeal—
Long have I labour'd for your common weal—
Long have I strove, unaided by the graces.
To spread good humour o'er your jolly faces.
    In short—to all it still shall be my pride,
Uncourtier like, tho' I have changed my side,
From Nature's source to act one favourite part,
To own your kindness with a grateful heart.

Among other complimentary effusions evoked by her appearance at Covent Garden was the following :—

      While Siddons melts the admiring town
        Each night without relief ;
      Ah ! where's my favourite Abington,
        To counteract this grief !
      Come then by kindred souls held dear,
        Your talents all employ,
      Siddons shall draw the pitying tear,
        You laugh us into joy.

December 6th, 1782, "The Way of the World," (not acted for six years at Covent Garden) Mrs. Abington as Millamant.

Dec. 20th, "The Sultan" (never acted there) Mrs. Abington as Roxalana.

Jan. 3rd, 1783, "All in the Wrong" (not acted for three years), Mrs. Abington as Belinda.

Jan. 17th, "The Capricious Lady," altered from "The Scornful Lady."

Elder Loveless...	WROUGHTON.
Young Loveless	LEWIS.
Welford, a suitor to the lady...	LEE LEWES.
Savil	QUICK.
Morecraft (an usurer)	WILSON.
Capricious Lady	MRS. ABINGTON.
Abigail, her woman	MRS. WEBB.
Martha, the lady's sister ...	MRS. LEWIS.
Widow	MRS. MORTON.

EPILOGUE TO THE CAPRICIOUS LADY.

Written by G. Colman, Esq.; and spoken by Mrs. Abington.

" In Fletcher's days it was the favourite plan
Of woman. to dethrone the tyrant man :
Our modern fashions vary—yet their aim,
Howe'er pursu'd. appears the very same.
The starch'd ruff'd maidens of Queen Bess's reign,
Were doomed a starch'd demeanor to maintain ;
Quill'd up like porcupines, they shot their darts,
Slaughter'd whole rows of knights, and wounded hearts :
Their virtue nought could shake, no siege could alter ;
A rock impregnable as Gibraltar :
In vain were sighs, and tears, and idle flattery,
Their red-hot balls laid low each hostile battery ;
While they bright stars. above all weak comparison,
Shone forth the female Elliots of the garrison.
    The modern maidens find things alter'd quite,
A hundred danglers, not one faithful knight ;
Nor coy. nor cruel, all her charms display'd,
Coldly she's seen ; and trusting, she's betray'd ;
Unfeeling coxcombs scorn the damsel's power,
And pass in Rotten-row the vacant hour.
The fair, her power thus lost in single life,
Reserves her policy till made a wife.
The humble married dames of Fletcher's day,
Thought wives must love. and honour, and obey ;
Bound in the nuptial ring, that hoop of gold
Enchain'd their passions and their will control'd.
Too oft the modern Miss, Scarce made a bride,

Breaks out at once all insolence, and pride :
Mounted in phaeton she courts the eye,
And, cats and games, and paints, and dresses high,
Who shall say nay? Content to drink, and play
His lordship cries—" My lady take your way,
I've fixt your box at the opera—but am vext
That Polly brilliant could not get the next."
    Such was the rigid line of ancient rule,
And such the freedom of the modern school ;
Choose which, ye fair, or else, to copy loth,
Compose a new *Pasticcio* out of both ;
Or smit with nobler pride, on Nature look,
And read the brightest pages of her book.
Would you a spotless maid, chaste wife be known,   )
Shew the young virtues rip'ning or full blown,   )
Mark how they prop, and dignify the throne ;   )
Rival their goodness, with a loyal strife,
And grace with royal virtues, private life.

According to accounts which have come down to us in the magazines of the period, Mrs. Abington had expressed a wish to appear in the character of the Scornful Lady in the play of that name; a part in which Mrs. Oldfield had been much celebrated, and which she is said to have performed with applause to the last. This comedy was therefore altered and brought out under the title of "The Capricious Lady," in which Mrs. Abington undertook the principal part; and though she had to contrast the cold, refined manners of the prude of the last century with the gay familiar habits of the present times (1783) she shewed that deep acumen in her profession, with the powers of exhibition so forcibly, that she rendered the Capricious Lady highly acceptable to the audience; who viewed it like one of the pictures of Vandyke, where beauty continues to be ever beautiful, however varied by the draperies of different ages.

‘ The alterations which were made by Mr. Cooke, a lawyer, and the omissions (for indeed there was much in the original which rendered it altogether unfit for public exhibition), were most judicious, and rendered the comedy tolerably well suited to the stage.

"For a dearth of wit which pervades the piece, great amends are made by comic humour. The dialogue is written with great feeling, and can easily be traced to Beaumont's pen. Upon the whole this comedy was favourably received and equally well performed, particularly the parts of Mrs. Abington and Mr. Wroughton, who entered into the real spirit of the author. The prologue was spoken by Mr. Lee Lewis, and the epilogue was delivered by Mrs. Abington with her usual vivacity; but they neither possessed any considerable share of merit to recommend them to the audience, notwithstanding the executions of both performers.

Feb. 19th, Mrs. Abington acted Beatrice.

April 25th, "The Maid of the Oaks," never acted before at Covent Garden, Mrs. Abington as Lady Bab Lardoon.

Jan. 23rd, 1784, "The Careless Husband," Mrs. Abington as Lady Betty Modish.

March 6th, "Rule a Wife," (not acted for four years) Mrs. Abington as Estifania.

On the 2nd of June, Covent Garden theatre closed for the season, when Mrs. Abington took leave of the town with the following address, written by herself:—

> "The play concluded, and this season o'er,
> When we shall view these friendly rows no more,
> In my *own character* let me appear,
> To pay my warmest, humblest, homage here ;
> Yet how shall words (those shadowy signs) reveal
> The real obligation which I feel ?
> Here they are fixed, and hence they ne'er shall part
> *While memory holds her seat* within my heart !
> This for myself.—Our friends and chief behind,
> Who bear your favours with a grateful mind,
> Have likewise bade me, as their proxy, own
> Your kind indulgence to their efforts shewn ;
> Efforts, which, warm'd by such a fost'ring choice,
> Again shall doubly court the public voice ;
> Till when, with duteous thanks, take our adieu,
> 'Tis meant to all, to you,* and you,† and you,‡
> Hoping to find you here in the same places, •
> With the same health, good spirits, and kind faces."

October 6th, "The Hypocrite" (not acted for twelve years) Mrs. Abington as Charlotte.

Nov. 11th, "The Way of the World," Mrs. Abington as Millamant.

March 5th, 1785, "The Way to Keep Him," (not acted for five years), Mrs. Abington as Widow Belmour.

Oct. 19th, "The Way to Keep Him," Mrs. A. as last time.

Nov. 2nd, "Much Ado," Mrs. Abington as Beatrice.

Nov. 7th, "The Suspicious Husband," Mrs. Abington as Clarinda.

Nov. 19th, "The Beaux Stratagem," Mrs. Abington as Mrs. Sullen.

      * Pit.   † Boxes.   ‡ Galleries.

Dec. 7th, " The Double Gallant," Mrs. Abington as Lady Sadlife.

Feb. 10th, 1786, Mrs. Abington's benefit. " The Beaux Stratagem," Scrub (for that night only), Mrs. Abington ; with " Three Weeks after Marriage." Pit and boxes were laid together. Ladies were desired to send their servants by four o'clock. Mrs. Abington is supposed to have acted.the part of Scrub for a wager, however that may be, it is evident that not-withstanding the full house she had, her conduct met with a deal of disapprobation. Almost universally she was considered to have fairly disgraced herself, and we constantly come across notices and criticisms in which she is roundly taken to task.

" Why am I obliged," writes Boaden, " to sully the fame of Abington by commemorating the utter and gross absurdity which led her to attempt the character of Scrub for her benefit ? The metamorphosis of her person, the loss of one sex, without approaching the other ; the coarse but vain attempt to vulgarise her voice, which some of my readers remember to have been thin, sharp and high-toned—all this ventured and producing nothing but disgust, I hope rendered the large receipt from the treasury itself less palatable than it had ever been upon any former occasion."

Then we have Mrs. Charles Mathews writing :—" Mrs. Abington (the original performer of Lady Teazle), in the latter portion of her dramatic life, was tempted to throw aside feminine grace and delicacy so far as to exhibit herself as Scrub in " The Beaux Stratagem," for her benefit—a character which, it may be said, she acted but too well. Grotesque portraits of her as this man-of-all-work are extant, and which might pass for tolerable likenesses of our inimitable Liston in the same character."

Russell says Peter Pindar thus alludes to this performance :—

" The courtly Abington's untoward star
Wanted her reputation much to mar,
And sink the lady to the washing tub—
So whisper'd, ' Mistress Abington, play Scrub.'
To folly full as great some imp may lug her,
And bid her sink in Fitch and Abel Drugger."

In allusion to this propensity of actors to figure in parts altogether unsuitable to them we cull the following from the Book of Theatrical Anecdotes :—

" Nearly all the great players have longed to figure in parts that were not suitable to their talents. The " comic countryman" of the provincial theatres often envies his brother professional in the part of Hamlet or Macbeth, and sincerely believes that he could do it more justice. Mrs. Siddons believed that she had great talents for comedy, acted the "Widow Brady," and once made a piteous exhibition of herself in Nell in "The Devil to Pay." She considered, too, that she could give a comic song called "Billy Taylor," with particular humour; and those who have heard her perform in this line declared that the grim and laborious solemnity was infinitely diverting. Her brother fancied that he shone in lively Charles Surface, which must have suggested something almost elephantine. King, the beau-ideal of high comedy, insisted on appearing as Richard the Third. The most outrageous exhibition of the kind was that of Mrs. Abington, the original, and said to have been the finest, Lady Teazle. At her benefit, to attract the town by the novelty of a new character, she performed the part of Scrub, in "The Beaux Stratagem." "At a very early hour," says Angelo, "the house was quite full. That night I accompanied my mother to Mrs. Garrick's box, when a general disappointment ensued. With all her endeavours to give new points to the character, she entirely failed. Her appearance *en cullottes*, so preposterously padded, exceeded nature. Her gestures to look comical could not get the least hold of the audience, though they had seen her before in men's clothes, when playing Portia, in "The Merchant of Venice," where her figure, dressed as a lawyer in his *gown*, gave effect to her excellent delivery on mercy, and the audience had always been delighted."

On this same evening when Mrs. Abington played Scrub, she also performed the part of Lady Racket in Murphy's "Three Weeks after Marriage;" she is said to have gone through the part of Scrub with her hair dressed for that of Lady Racket.

Spoken by Mrs. Abington, in the character of Lady Racket on her benefit night, Feb. 10th, 1786:

> "The world's a pantomime, and every man
> Is Harlequin as much as e'er he can;
> Mask'd with hypocrisy, and arm'd with cunning,
> In motley garb through endless mazes running
> With Columbine along. And who is she?
> But each man's giddy mistress—Vanity!
> For her assuming each fantastic shape,
> No matter what—of fopling or of ape.
> Well—ye have all your passions, and 'tis mine,
> (Call it my hobby, or my Columbine)
> Wrapp'd in your graciousness to play my part

Whilst *honest gratitude* expands my heart,
This is my dear delight, and, warm'd by this,
No shape of comic humour comes amiss."
Pertness, absurdity, or affectation,
Are things alike of comic imitation;
Be theirs the censure, but, if we excel,
Be ours the praise of imitating well;
Let Shakespear shield us, he delighted more
To stoop at mirthful follies than to soar.
Well then, let writers print and malice grin,
This night we've boldly vied with Harlequin.
Changing (a change it seems of special note)
These lady vestments for a butler's coat,
But you approving, we defy each grub,
And Racket rises undebas'd by Scrub.

Feb. 22nd, "The West Indian," Mrs. Abington as Charlotte Rusport.

March 11th, "Conscious Lovers," Mrs. Abington as Phillis.

This season Mrs. Abington re-visited Ireland and made an engagement to play for fifteen nights, for the sum of £500. In July (1786) she published the following card at Dublin.

"The very flattering partiality Mrs. Abington has experienced on her present visit to this kingdom, as well as upon every former occasion, calls forth such warm sensations of gratitude, as makes her anxious to seize the earliest opportunity of making her acknowledgments in the most respectful manner, for such repeated marks of favour from a generous indulgent public: she takes occasion at the same time to acknowledge that every endeavour was exerted on the part of Mr. Daly to make her situation as agreeable in the theatre as could possibly result from the most friendly and polite attention."

Feb. 7th, 1787, "The Provoked Husband," Mrs. Abington as Lady Townly.

March 15th, "The Way to Keep Him," Mrs. Abington as the Widow Belmour.

March 31st, Lewis' benefit, "The Careless Husband," Mrs. Abington as Lady Betty Modish.

April 30th, "The Miser," not acted ten years, Mrs. Abington as Lappet.

Nov. 7th, "Much Ado," Mrs. Abington as Beatrice.

Dec. 5th, "The Tender Husband," never acted there, Mrs. Abington as Biddy Tipkin.

G

Dec. 10th, "The Inconstant," not acted for eight years, Mrs. Abington as Bisarre.

Jan. 2nd, 1788, "The Suspicious Husband," Mrs. Abington as Clarinda.

April 14th, Mrs. Abington's benefit; she appeared as Kitty, in "High Life Below Stairs." A mock minuet by Ryder and Mrs. Abington.

Jan. 8th, 1789, "The Hypocrite," Mrs. Abington's first appearance this season.

Jan. 20th, "Much Ado," Mrs. Abington as Beatrice.

Jan. 23rd, Mrs. A—— acted Estifania.

Feb. 24th, "Conscious Lovers," Phillis, Mrs. Abington.

March 5th, "Old Batchelor," Mrs. Abington as Letitia.

April 2nd, "Sultan," Roxalana, Mrs. Abington.

May 8th, "School for Wives," Charlotte Richmore, Mrs. Abington.

May 18th, "Beggar's Opera," Lucy, Mrs Abington.

Nov. 5th, "Hypocrite," Mrs. A——'s first appearance this season.

Dec. 11th, "Way to Keep Him," Widow Belmour, Mrs. Abington.

Between 1790 and 1797 Mrs. Abington was absent from the stage, and it was generally supposed her professional life was at an end. Efforts however were made to induce her again to make her appearance in public, though we believe it was her fixed determination not to do so.

She had many allurements to this choice; a first rate and long established reputation in her profession; a genteel independency; and with these a circle of the most respectable characters in literary and polished life, constantly soliciting her society. In short, all the charms of the *otium cum dignitate* presented themselves, when *accident*, which perhaps determines us more in the affairs of life than rules drawn from reflection, decided otherwise.

The late Glorious Naval Victory, obtained by the Earl of St. Vincent over the Spanish Fleet, at the same time that it revived the well known ardour of the British nation, drew forth its utmost liberality; the widows and orphans of those men who so bravely and nobly fell in the defence of their country, that country felt for, honoured, and rewarded. Subscriptions were immediately opened for their relief, when all ranks of society pressed forward as their benefactors. Amongst the rest, the Manager of Covent Garden, with his usual liberality, gave a free night, and the first performers of both theatres as liberally offered their services.

In a contest of generous feeling, it was far, very far from the character of Abington to be an idle spectator. Though she had seemingly quitted the field of glory, and her suspended banners triumphantly proclaimed her former services, she could not resist the alluring bait of making her talents serviceable to the cause of humanity. She wrote to his Grace the Duke of Leeds, as one of the trustees for managing the charity, offering to speak an Epilogue on the occasion, or to come forward in any other shape where she could be of most advantage. The former was politely and readily accepted, and she spoke the Epilogue amidst the unbounded applause of a most numerous and brilliant audience. This was on June 14th, 1797.

This circumstance of course occasioned an interview with the manager, who took this opportunity to press her return to the stage. Other incidents strengthened this solicitation : the death of the late Mrs. Pope (who, as an *actress* or a *woman*, must be ever mentioned with respect), with the retirement of Miss Wallis, &c., created a chasm in the arrangements of the theatre, which none but extraordinary talents could fill up: the manager saw his remedy in Mrs. Abington; and Mrs. Abington might have seen from this and other circumstances, that she might accomodate herself more in the line of her business now than heretofore. Whatever were her motives, after some hesitation, she accepted the manager's offer, and soon after the opening of the theatre, she made her appearance in Beatrice, introduced by a prologue, written by Mr. Colman for that purpose, and spoken by Murray. This was on the 6th of October.

> " Whene'er the mind assumes a pensive cast,
> And Memory sits musing on the past ;
> When Melancholy counts each friend gone by,
> True as Religion strings her rosary,
> The eye grows moist for many in silence laid,
> And drops that bead which Nature's self has made.
> To friends alone, then, is the tear-drop due ?
> Oh, no ! to public virtue—Genius too :
> Fondly we dwell on merit Death has cross'd,
> On talent we have witness'd, and have lost.
> Here, on this mimic scene, alas the day !
> How many fleeting time has snatch'd away !
> His fatal scythe, of late, the hoary sage
> Has swung with ampler sweep along the stage.

Tardy no more, he treads the Drama's ground,
But strides like Mars, and mows with fury round.

Companions of his course, on either hand,
Death glares—and gentle Hymen waves his brand.
Here Death to a chill grave some actor carries,
Here Hymen beckons—and an actress marries.
Thinn'd thus, of brilliant talent, and of worth,
Is then our Drama threaten'd with a dearth?
Not so, we trust—for judgment sure can find
Full many a favourite still left behind.
Many, whose industry and modest sense
Your smiles have mellow'd into excellence;
Whose sparks of merit, fann'd into a flame
By Candour's breath, now kindle into fame.
And if, while glancing o'er Thalia's ground,
The critic eye some casual void has found,
Can she not fill the chasm in her train,
And lure some favour'd vot'ry back again?
E'en now the Muse on high her banners rears;
Thalia calls—and ABINGTON appears:
Yes, ABINGTON—too long we've been without her,
With all the school of Garrick still about her.
Mature in pow'rs, in playful fancy vernal—
For Nature, charming Nature, is eternal.
And, oh! while now a favourite returns,
Whose breast for you with grateful passion burns,
Keep up Thalia's cause!—scorn, scorn to drop it!—
And cheer her Priestess, who now comes to prop it."

Her reception from the public was such as did honour to both parties: she was welcomed with shouts of unbounded applause, which she evidently felt with respect and gratitude. Those who had never seen her before (for such is the fluctuating state of human nature, that a few years make a considerable change in the formation of audience) were surprised at the appearance of an actress, whom the little pens of malice had been previously endeavouring to sink into age and necessary retirement, in the full possession of person, health, and talents; whilst those of her former dramatic admirers hailed her like the morn " after a winter's return of light." They saw their favourite comic actress again restored to them in the full meridian of abilities, with Shakspeare, Congreve, Vanburgh, Wycherly, and "all the muses in her train."

This celebrated actress was now, beyond doubt, getting into years, though she was ever we are told, particularly desirous of being thought younger than she really was, accordingly it is not surprising to find her declining to recite in public the following lines which a writer of the times composed for her on her return to professional life :—

" Yes, my loved patrons! I am here once more,
Though many kindly say that I'm fourscore ;
Perhaps you think so, and with wonder see
That I can curtsey thus with pliant knee ;
That still without two crutches I am walking,
And, what's more strange, don't mumble in my talking."

She never took any formal farewell of the public, nor did she have, as many others have had, a farewell benefit, but she made her last appearance on the stage at Covent Garden, on the 12th of April, 1799, as Lady Racket, in "Three Weeks after Marriage," for the benefit of Pope, her old companion in many seasons.

She was afterwards solicited by a near relative of a gentleman who had done her much service in his newspaper, to act for her benefit, to which she replied as follows :—

AUGUST 26TH, 1801.

My dear Madam,—The obligation, I am proud to say I owe to Mr. —— for the indulgent partiality with which he has been pleased to distinguish my exertions in my profession, call upon me for every acknowledgment that gratitude and sensibility can inspire.

It is, therefore, with infinite mortification that I find myself under the necessity of refusing the request made to me in your very polite and very interesting letter ; and I trust, my dear Madam, that I shall stand excused in your opinion, when I assure you that if it were given me to choose whether I would go upon the stage or beg charity from my friends, for my daily bread, I would embrace the latter condition, and think myself a gainer in credit by the preference.

In this state of mind you cannot be surprised at my declining a visit to Brighton ; but I must not conclude my letter without saying that there is a passage in yours which I do not understand : it seems to convey an idea that I have recently been (somehow or other) of use to your father. I would to God it had been in my power, either now or at any other preceding period of my life, to show my gratitude for his infinite goodness and friendship to me ; but hitherto this power has been denied to me and it is only in poverty of words, as well as circumstances, that I have been able to acknowledge my many, many obligati,ons.

My spirits are very much hurt while I am writing upon this subject ; you must, therefore, permit me to conclude with my acknowledgments to Mr. ——, and believe me, my dear Madam,
Your most obedient and very humble servant,
F. ABINGTON.

She lived until the year 1815, when, on March 4th, she died at her apartments in Pall Mall, in good circumstances, her husband, to whom she allowed a handsome annuity, having died some nine years previously, the money, in consequence, reverting to herself. It is said, however, that she lost a good deal of money by gambling with cards, a vice to which ladies of fashion and quality were then much addicted.

With regard to Mrs. Abington's merits as an actress, Dibdin in his "History of the Stage," thus writes :—

"With Mrs. Abington came a species of excellence which the stage seems never before to have boasted in the same perfection. The higher parts in comedy had been performed chastely and truly, perhaps in these particulars more so than by this actress, There was a peculiar goodness gleamed across the levity of Mrs. Pritchard, and by what one can learn of Mrs. Bracegirdle, who seems to have possessed the same captivating sort of manner which distinguished Mrs. Abington, she was in those characters natural and winning; but it remained for her successor to add a degree of grace, fashion, and accomplishment to sprightliness, which was no sooner seen than it was imitated in the politest circles.

Mrs. Bracegirdle, let her merit have been what it might, did not perform Cibber's Coquettes, and though that author waited for Mrs. Oldfield before he accomplished Lady Betty Modish, yet however admirable she might have been in the representation of those characters, they did not appear to be so exactly in her way as Lady Townly and other parts which had a higher degree of consequence attached to them.

Mrs. Abington kept critically to coquettes, and there can be no doubt, take the round of them through, and it is pretty extensive, that more uniform good acting never was manifested.

I have already spoken comparatively of Mrs. Abington and Madame Bellcour, but with no views to associate them in elegance and grace, which the characters Madame Bellcour personated would not in the same degree admit of. The French actress personated French coquettes to admiration, but I have already observed, speaking of King and Preville, that everything among the French is underwritten. They know nothing of Beatrice, Lady Betty Modish, or Millamant. The likeness is in those higher kinds of chambermaids who aped their mistresses, and thus exactly as we have been accustomed to say King and Abington, instead of Tom and Phillis, so it was impossible to speak of Preville without assimilating the idea of Bellcour.

In addition to the grace, the ease, and elegance with which Mrs. Abington personated characters in high life, and aped politeness in chambermaids, her taste for dress was novel and interesting. She was consulted by ladies of the first distinction, not from caprice as we have frequently seen in other instances, but from a decided conviction of her judgment in blending what was beautiful with what was becoming. Indeed dress took a sort of ton from her fancy, and ladies both on the stage and off, piqued themselves on decorating their persons with decency and decorum, and captivating beholders by a modest concealment of those charms, which, in imitation of the French women, who never knew the sensation of a blush, the result of English feminine rectitude, our females now, to the disgrace of the age, make it their study to expose."

SHAKESPEARE AND ABINGTON.

"It is a matter of solid satisfaction to every friend to the Drama, that Mrs. Abington has been brought back to the stage, not merely on account of her own extraordinary and unrivalled talents, but because her cast of parts lies chiefly in the dramatic personæ of those writers who have been uniformly deemed by men of general learning, critical taste and acknowledged judgment, the ornaments of the time in which they lived, and the great supporters of the stage, by the force, variety, and excellence of their dramatic productions. Shakespeare, Beaumont and Fletcher, and Congreve, are the authors, in whose plays she has most powerfully evinced her knowledge of her profession, and established her high character as a comedian. In this age of frivolity and folly, when caricature and eccentricty threaten to bear down truth and nature, and already almost put common sense out of countenance, will not every friend to the drama seriously rejoice that the return of Mrs. Abington, in its first instance, may be considered as an appeal to the audience to an effect similar to that of Dr. Johnson, in the following lines in his celebrated Prologue, spoken by Mr. Garrick on opening the theatre in Drury-lane, in 1747!"

"'Tis yours this night to bid the reign commence,
Of rescued nature and reviving sense."

"Much Ado about Nothing" has some of Shakespeare's richest bullion in it, blended with an alloy of base metal, but neither one nor the other are unworthy of that great master from whose mint they were issued, and who well knew that without some alloy the purest one could not be rendered current.

In Beatrice, Mrs. Abington shewed how thoroughly she entered into the author's design, and that his rich vein of wit was her familiar acquaintance, not a new one ; that they met on the terms of long friendship, and walked and talked together with all the ease and elegance of persons of congenial minds and similar manners.   No forced archness, no affectation of conceiving more than the expression naturally conveyed, was suffered to mar the beauty of a single scene.   The auditor merely read Shakespeare with his ear and not his eye, but he read him more accurately, and, if possible, with better effect. In point of figure Mrs. Abington is more *en bon point* than when she last appeared as an actress, and she certainly is not younger, but she has not lost one atom of her judgment ; on the contrary it is evidently improved ; neither is her power of manifesting her pretentions to an eminent superiority in skill, as well as science in her profession, to most of her competitors, in the smallest degree diminished.   In fact she proved the truth of the line applied to her with so much approbation in Mr. Colman's well written address, which announces her as

"Mature in powers, in playful fancy vernal."

She dressed Beatrice finely, and perhaps the critic may say she was somewhat too fine ; but it must be remembered, the dress of Beatrice is *ad libitum*, and Mrs. Abington could not better pay her court to her best friends, than by appearing *parfaitement habile.*

Mr. Lewis played the part of Benedick with great truth, spirit, and character,—a circumstance equally gratifying and astonishing, considering how much within these few years, he has lent himself to folly, and been the distinguished hero of extravagance : in fact, he has seemed so happy, and exhibited so much adroitness in breaking a chair and tossing up a candle-stick, to the great danger of his fellow-comedians' pericraniums, that the writer of this article, in common with others, thought him not only a truant to Shakespeare, but should have imagined him an absolute deserter from his standard, had not he occasionally proved, by the pleasant energy of his Mercutio, and some other of Shakespeare's characters, that he still paid due homage to his liege Lord, and was eager to shew his zeal, when occasion required.   His Benedick was a full refutation of the calumnies of those who made no scruple to assert that Lewis was spoiled as a comedian.. He played the character chastely, forcibly, and with great effect.

The audience did themselves honour by their kind notice of

Mr. Hull, in Antonio: they could not act more liberally or more creditably than by cheering an old servant, always respectable, both on the stage and in private life.

Mrs. Abington's recent performances completely realize the epigram of

"Ancient Phyllis has young graces."

Davies, in his "Life of Garrick," says:

"It is with the greatest pleasure I speak of Mrs. Abington's action in Charlotte: though the part had been most excellently performed by Mrs. Oldfield, and since her time with great applause and approbation by Mrs. Woffington and Mrs. Pritchard: yet it is impossible to conceive that more gaiety, ease, humour, elegance, and grace, could have been assumed by any actress than by Mrs. Abington in this part; her ideas of it were entirely her own, for she had seen no pattern.

But the various talents of Mrs. Abington will demand from a stage historian particular attention, and a more accurate description of them. Her person is formed with great elegance, her address is graceful, her look animated and expressive. To the goodness of her understanding, and the superiority of her taste, she is indebted principally for her power of pleasing; the tones of her voice are not naturally charming to the ear, but her incomparable skill in modulation renders them perfectly agreeable: her articulation is so exact, that every syllable she utters is conveyed distinctly and even harmoniously. Congreve's Millamant of past times she has skilfully modelled and adapted to the admired coquette and the lonely tyrant of the present day. All ages have their particular colours and variations of follies and fashions; these she understands perfectly and dresses them to the taste of the present hour. In Shakespeare's Beatrice she had difficulties to encounter and prejudices to conquer: remembrance of Mrs. Pritchard's excellence in that favourite part, had stamped a decisive mark as her mode of representing it; notwithstanding this, Mrs. Abington, knowing her own particular powers of expression, would not submit to an imitation of that great actress, but exhibited the part according to her own ideas; nor did she fail of gaining great applause wherever her judgment directed her to point out the wit, sentiment, or humour of Beatrice.

In the Widow Belmour of Murphy's "Way to Keep Him," her disengaged and easy manner, familiar to one who had been used to the company of persons distinguished by high rank and graceful behaviour, rendered her the delight of a brilliant circle

of admirers.   In Lady Bab Lardoon, the author of " The Maid
of the Oaks " has, in a very delicate strain of panegyric, paid a
lasting tribute to her merit.   When this lady of high life, to
impose on Dupley, a young travelling coxcomb, assumes a
character of great simplicity, and tries her skill at a little
naivete; she says to one who is a witness of the diversion; " You
shall see what an excellent actress I should have made, if fortune
had not unluckily brought me into the world an earl's daughter."
This elegant compliment needs no comment.

Though the theatre would have been almost deprived of the
accomplished and well-bred woman of fashion, without the
assistance of Mrs. Abington, yet so various and unlimited are
her talents, that she is not confined to females of a superior
class ; she can descend occasionally to the country girl, the romp,
the hoyden, and the chambermaid, and put on the various
humours, airs, and whimsical peculiarities of these under parts.
She thinks nothing low that is in nature ; nothing mean or
beneath her skill, which is characteristical.

The decency of her behaviour in private life has attracted the
notice and gained her the esteem of many persons of quality of
her own sex.   Like another Oldfield or Cibber, she receives visits
from, and returns them, to ladies of the most distinguished
worth and the highest rank.   Her taste in dress is allowed to be
superior, and she is often consulted in the choice of fashionable
ornaments by her female friends in high life ; but as it would be
absurd to confine her merit to so trifling an accomplishment,
she cannot be denied the praise of engaging and fixing the
regard of all her acquaintance by her good sense, elegance of
manner, and propriety of conduct.

EPILOGUE TO THE MINIATURE PICTURE.

Spoken by Mrs. Abington, at Drury-lane.

The men, like tyrants of the Turkish kind,
Have long our sex's energy confin'd;
In full dress black, and bows, and solemn stalk,
Have long monopoliz'd the Prologue's walk.
But still the flippant epilogue was ours;
It asked for gay support—the female powers ;
It ask'd a stirring air, coquet and free ;
And so to murder it, they fix'd on Me.
Much they mistake my talents—I was born
To tell in sobs and sighs, some tale forlorn ;
To wet my handkerchief with Juliet's woes,
Or tune to Shore's despair my tragic nose.

Yes, gentlemen, in education's spite,
You still shall find that we can read and write;
Like you can swell a debt or a debate,
Can quit the card-table to steer the State;
Or bid our Belle Assemblée's rhet'ric flow,
To drown your dull declaimers at Soho.
Methinks, e'en now, I hear my sex's tongues
The shrill, smart melody of female lungs!
The storm of question, the division calm,
With "Hear her! hear her! Mrs. Speaker, Ma'am!
Oh, Order! Order!"—Kates and Susans rise,
And Marg'ret moves, and Tabitha replies.
Look to the camp—Coxheath and Warley Common
Supplied at least for ev'ry tent a woman.
The cartridge-paper wrapped the billet-doux,
The rear and picquet formed the rendez-vous.
The drum's stern rattle shook the nuptial bed;
The knapsack pillow'd Lady Sturgeon's head.
Love was the watchword, till the morning fife
Rous'd the tame Major and his warlike wife.
Look to the Stage.   To-night's example draws
A female dramatist to grace the cause.
So fade the triumphs of presumptuous man!
And would you, Ladies, but complete my plan,
Here would ye sign some "patriot petition,"
To mend our "constitutional" condition.
The men invade our rights—the mimic elves
Lisp and nickname God's creatures, ourselves;
Rouge more than we do, simper, flounce, and fret,
And they coquet, good Gods! how they coquet!
They too are coy; and monstrous to relate!
Theirs is the coyness in a *tête-a-tête.*
Yes, Ladies, yes, "I could a tale unfold,"
"Would harrow up your"—cushions were it told;
Part your combined curls, and freeze—pomatum,
At griefs and grievances, as I could state 'em.
"But such eternal blazon must not" speak—
Besides, the house adjourns some day next week.—
This fair "Committee" shall detail the rest,
Then let the monsters (if they dare) protest!

EPILOGUE TO ZENOBIA.

Written by D. Garrick; Spoken by Mrs. Abington.
[*She peeps through the Curtain.*]

How do you all good folks? In tears for certain
I'll only take a *peep behind the curtain;*
You're all so full of tragedy and sadness!
For me to come among ye, would be madness

This is no time for giggling—when you've leisure,
Call out for me and I'll attend your pleasure;
As soldiers hurry at the beat of drum,
Beat but your hands, that instant I will come.

[*She enters upon their clapping.*]

This is so good to call me out so soon—
The Comic muse by me intreats a *boon*;
She call'd for *Prichard*, her first maid of honour,
And begg'd of her to take the task upon her;
But she,—I'm sure you'll all be sorry for't,
Resigns her place and soon retires from court:
To bear this loss we courtiers make a shift,
When good folks leave us, worse may have a lift.
The *Comic muse* whose every smile is grace ⎞
And her *Stage sister*, with her tragic face, ⎬
Have had a quarrel—each has writ a case ⎠
And on their friends assembled now I wait,
To give you of *their difference a true state*
Melpomene, complains when she appears,—
For five good acts, in all her pomp of tears,
To raise your souls, and with her raptures wing 'em;
Nay wet your handkerchiefs that you may wring 'em.
Some flippant hussey like myself comes in;
Crack goes her fan, and with a giggling grin,
Hey! Presto! pass!—all topsy turvy see,
For bo, bo, bo! is chang'd to be, be, be!
We own the fault, but 'tis a fault in vogue,
'Tis theirs, who call and brawl for—Epilogue!
O! Shame upon you—for the time to come,
Know better, and go miserable home.
What says our *Comic goddess?*—With reproaches,
She vows her *Sister Tragedy* encroaches!
And spite of all her virtue and ambition,
Is known to have an am'rous disposition;
For in *False Delicacy*—wondrous fly,
Join'd with a certain Irishman—O fye!
She made you, when you ought to laugh, to cry.
Her sister's smiles with tears she tried to smother, ⎞
Rais'd such a tragi-comic kind of pother, ⎬
You laugh'd with one eye, while you cried with t'other. ⎠
What can be done?—sad work behind the scenes!
These comic females scold with tragic queens;
Each party different ways the foe assails,
These shake their daggers, those prepare their nails.
'Tis you alone must calm these dire mishaps,
Or we shall still continue pulling caps.
What is your will?—I read it in your faces; ⎞
That all hereafter take their proper places, ⎬
Shake hands, and kiss, and friends, and—burn their cases. ⎠

IMPROMPTU.

See the bills once more grac'd with an Abington's name;
Is she led into public by interest or fame?
Their dictates this offspring of Nature has scorn'd
For her cot is by taste and contentment adorn'd;
They have breath'd soft tranquility's charms on her mind
And the mask of *Thalia* she long has resigned.
Then what has induc'd her again to engage
In theatric toils and appear on the Stage?
Meek Charity came and the Nymph thus addrest
"O wouldst thou by widows and orphans be blest!
"Behold with compassion this sorrowing train:
"O Abington! can they solicit in vain?
Sad relics of those who by Jervis the brave,
"Were embalm'd with his sighs e're they sunk in the wave;
"He saw them, undaunted, fight long by his side,
"And his heart felt a pang for each hero that died,
"To their mem'ry by thee let a Tribute be paid;
"Forego thine own ease, and this night deign to aid
"The endeavours of those who benignly come forth,
"And from Penury's hand strive to extricate worth;
"Exert thy known talents in pleading a cause
"So *glorious* that *Heaven* will give thee applause."

ODE

On Mrs. Abington's Return to the Stage.

As at reviving morn the Persian bows,
Drops his white hand and offers up his vows,
While glowing Phœbus marching through the skies,
Gilds the bright mosque, and glitters in his eyes;
Should some dark cloud obscure the blue serene,
Damps chill the air, or tempests intervene,
No more the eye of Joy emits a ray,
Sad is the hour and listless is the day.
But if again the glorious sun appears,
Lost are his sighs, and fruitless are his fears;
Fervour anew reanimates his breast,
And all his hopes, his passions, are confess'd.
   Thus, thus, when wit and native beauty shone,
Depicted to the world in Abington,
The all that Fancy from her stores could shew
That Wit might ask for, or that Wit bestow;
Ease, elegance, the artless charm to please,
The elegance of art, the art of ease:
Such were her powers, by judgment such confess'd,
And those that knew them most, rever'd them best.
Lost for a while, no more can Shakspeare glow,
Thalia weeps the *vivifying bow—*

No promis'd hope—the age of Wit is o'er,
Genius is lost, and Fancy is no more.
Desponding Care, and Caution, hence away,
Again returns reiterated day.
Once more the Queen of smiles her seat assumes,
And every face that boasts of sense illumes.
Hail her kind Genius, Guardian of the Stage,
The test of thought, the pleasure of the age.
  Hail her, hail her! Nymphs attend,
  Hail her, sweetest Shakspeare's friend;
  Bard that wrote from Nature's eye,
  To clothe her with his livery.
  What was plaintive, solemn, sad,
  What in cheerful garb was clad,
  Thoughts at first obscure in meaning,
  Or lost from inattentive gleaning,
  By Abington are richly dress'd,
  And what seem'd poor appear the best.
  The linsey garb, the ermin'd fur,
  Alike are costly robes on her;
  Sole empress on Thalia's throne,
  For Nature deigns to put them on.
When through the drear opaque a ray is seen,
Clouds break on clouds, and light is caught between,
Hope brings a comfort with the beaming ray,
Again to gild the honorary day;
Once more a prospect to the Stage is shewn,
When Abington resumes Thalia's throne!

TASTE.

To Mrs. Abington.

Say my blythe Frances whither must I go
To meet respect or extirpate my woe,
See how my Ministry neglected lie,
Now you've receded from the publick eye,
Let reciprocity our wills combine,
I will be your ally, and you be mine,
Like correspondent benefits we'll live,
You shall bestow, while I am proud to give.
Then come, ah! come, and cheer me with thy voice,
That fashion may exult, and social life rejoice.

Thalia droops, and weeps amid her bowers,
See vulgar arrogance annoys her hours,
Say shall that Nymph who dignified your name
Be smote by worthless hands or lose her fame,
Ere you departed, she was proud to own,
My cheerful race, and led them to her Throne,
Then Phœbus beam'd all glorious on the throng
While you upheld my rights, and sanctified my song,
Then all the sister Muses gladly blest,
Their infant offspring and their arts carest.

On Mrs. Abington's excellent Performance of Lady Rentless,
in the new Comedy of Dissipation.

Would you know what is *fashion*, ye young and ye fair,
Who think it consists in *fine clothes* and *fine hair*,
Or *singing*, or *dancing*, without *ear* or *taste*,
Or *drawling the language*, or *lacing the waist*,
Let Abington teach !—Tis that happy skill,
To exhibit a grace when you move or stand still,
To attract by the *choice of your dress*, not by *glaring* ;
To hear *without wonder*, and see *without staring* ;
To speak from the passions, by manners refined,
Nor *noisy*, nor *mincing*, nor *coarse*, nor *confined*,
In short, if of *fashion*, you'd have a full sample,
'Tis that the best shews, by her *own great example*.

To Mrs. ABINGTON.

STRAWBERRY HILL, JUNE 11TH, 1780.

You may certainly always command me and my house. My
common custom is to give a ticket for only four persons at a
time ; but it would be very insolent in me, when all laws are
set at naught, to pretend to prescribe rules. At such times there
is a shadow of authority in setting the laws aside by the
legislature itself ; and though I have no army to supply their
place, I declare Mrs. Abington may march through all my
dominions at the head of as large a troop as she pleases—I do
not say, as she can muster and command ; for then I am sure
my house would not hold them. The day, too, is at her own
choice ; and the master is her very obedient humble servant,

HOR. WALPOLE.

EPILOGUE,

Written by Mr. Garrick, and spoken by Mrs. Abington.

[*Enters in a hurry.*]

Forgive my coming thus our griefs to utter—
I'm such a figure !—and in such a flutter—
So circumstanced, in such an awkard way
I know not what to do, or what to say.
Our Bard, a strange unfashionable creature,
As obstinate as savage in his nature,
Will have no Epilogue !—I told the brute—
If, Sir, these trifles don't *your* genius suit ;

We have a working Prologue-smith within,
Will strike one off as if it were a pin.
Nay, Epilogues are pins,—whose points, well plac'd,
Will trick your muse out, in the tip-top taste!
' Pins, madam ! (frown'd the Bard) the Greeks us'd none,⎫
' Then mutt'ring Greek—something like this—went on⎬
' *Pinnos, painton, pa beros, non Græco Modon.*'⎭
I coax'd, he swore—' That tie him to a stake,
' He'd suffer all for decency's fair sake ;
' No bribery should make him change his plan.'
There's an odd mortal.   Match him if you can.
Hah, Sir ! (said I)—your reasoning is not deep,⎫
For when at Tragedies spectators weep,⎬
They oft, like children cry themselves to sleep.⎭
And if no jogging Epilogue you write,
Pit, Box, and Gallery may sleep all night.
' Better (he swore)—a nap should overtake ye,
' Than folly should to folly's pranks awake ye:
' Rakes are more harmless nodding upon benches,
' Than ogling to insnare poor simple wenches ;
' And simple girls had better close their eyes,
' Than send 'em gadding after butterflies.
' Nay, should a Statesman make a box his nest,
' Who, that his country loves, would break his rest ?
' Let come what may, I will not make 'em laugh ;
' Take for an *Epilogue*—This *Epitaph* ;
' For as my lovers live I would not save,
' No pois'nous weeds shall root upon their grave.'
'Tis thus these pedant Greek-read poets vapour—
Is it your pleasure I should read the paper ?

   Here, in the arms of death, a matchless pair,
A young-lov'd hero, and beloved fair,
Now find repose—Their virtues tempest-tost,
Sea-sick, and weary, reach the wish'd-for coast,
Whatever mortal to this spot is brought,
O may the living by the dead be taught!
May here Ambition learn to clip her wing,
And Jealousy to blunt her deadly sting ;
Then shall the Poet every wish obtain,
Nor Ronan and Rivine die in vain.

————

VERSES,

*On seeing Mrs. Abbington perform Lady Bab Lardoon, at the
Request of her Grace the Duchess of Marlborough.*

    Behold, illustrious Marlborough appears,
    Whom Virtue honours, and whom Taste reveres ;
    She comes with Youth and Beauty at her side,
    To see the Comic Muse in all her pride ;

By elegance her fav'rite handmaid drest,
Sportive Thalia meets her noble guest;
With native dignity she trips along,
Attendant graces round her person throng;
By her with modish gaiety's display'd
The polish'd manners of the high born maid:
The rustic playfulness, and artless ease,
Her Philly Nettletop is sure to please;
Simplex munditiis charms throughout the whole,
And more than Lady Bab enchants the soul.

If, when at Blenheim, lovely Spencer deigns
To grace, with sprightly mirth, these mimic scenes,
In the first character herself she'll find.
At home, in all, but errors of the mind:
And in the rural beauty of the vale,
Such charming innocence can never fail;
If nature's easy dictates she'll pursue,
A perfect model we in each shall view;
Thalia will the wreath of fame resign;
And round fair Spencer's brows the chaplet twine.

IMPROMPTU,

On seeing Mrs. Abington in the very contrasted Characters of
Lady Bab Lardoon and Philly Nettletop, in
"The Maid of the Oaks."

Nature and Fashion now no more
Shall disagree as heretofore,
 But both their force unite,
Convinc'd one female can display
Th' extended pow'rs of either's sway,
 And variegate delight.

Where is the female? Envy cries,
Lo, Abington! she'll teach your eyes
 And heart—this truth to know:
In Lady Bab such graces aid,
In Nettletop—just such a maid
 As Arcady could shew.

INDEX.

www.ingramcontent.com/pod-product-compliance
Lightning Source LLC
Chambersburg PA
CBHW032015010726

47493CB00007B/2414